HERE COMES
THE SHAGGEDY

GOOSEBUMPS®

NIGHT OF THE LIVING DUMMY
DEEP TROUBLE
MONSTER BLOOD
THE HAUNTED MASK
ONE DAY AT HORRORLAND
THE CURSE OF THE MUMMY'S TOMB
BE CAREFUL WHAT YOU WISH FOR
SAY CHEESE AND DIE!
THE HORROR AT CAMP JELLYJAM
HOW I GOT MY SHRUNKEN HEAD
THE WEREWOLF OF FEVER SWAMP
A NIGHT IN TERROR TOWER
WELCOME TO DEAD HOUSE
WELCOME TO CAMP NIGHTMARE
GHOST BEACH
THE SCARECROW WALKS AT MIDNIGHT
YOU CAN'T SCARE ME!
RETURN OF THE MUMMY
REVENGE OF THE LAWN GNOMES
PHANTOM OF THE AUDITORIUM
VAMPIRE BREATH
STAY OUT OF THE BASEMENT
A SHOCKER ON SHOCK STREET
LET'S GET INVISIBLE!
NIGHT OF THE LIVING DUMMY 2
NIGHT OF THE LIVING DUMMY 3
THE ABOMINABLE SNOWMAN OF PASADENA
THE BLOB THAT ATE EVERYONE
THE GHOST NEXT DOOR
THE HAUNTED CAR
ATTACK OF THE GRAVEYARD GHOULS
PLEASE DON'T FEED THE VAMPIRE

ALSO AVAILABLE:

IT CAME FROM OHIO!: MY LIFE AS A WRITER by R.L. Stine

HERE COMES
THE SHAGGEDY

R.L. STINE

SCHOLASTIC INC.

Goosebumps book series created by Parachute Press, Inc.
Copyright © 2016 by Scholastic Inc.

ISBN 978-0-545-82547-4

10 9 8 7 6 5   16 17 18 19 20

Printed in the U.S.A.   40
First printing 2016

WELCOME. YOU ARE MOST WANTED.

Come right in. I'm R.L. Stine. Welcome to the Goosebumps office.

You're just in time for lunch. Let me wipe the hair off that spoon so you can share my soup with me. Sorry. I was using the spoon to feed my chimpanzee.

Do you like black bean soup? I like it a lot, but there's one thing I don't understand. Why are the beans moving around in the bowl? It's hard to eat things that keep moving — don't you agree? (I've never seen beans with legs before!)

I see you are admiring the WANTED posters on the wall. Those posters show the creepiest, crawliest, grossest Goosebumps characters of all time. They are the MOST WANTED characters from the MOST WANTED books.

That poster you are studying is of a mythical swamp creature called the Shaggedy. He's just a legend. He's not real. The only problem is, no one explained that to the Shaggedy.

1

Here are Kelli and Shawn Andersen. When they moved to the Florida swamps, it didn't take them long to find out if the Shaggedy was real or not.

Go ahead. Read their story. It isn't pretty. You will soon understand why the Shaggedy is MOST WANTED.

1

The swamp at night makes trickling sounds, gurgling, popping. The river water is alive, and the sand shifts and moves as if it's restless. The chitter and whistle of insects never stops. Birds flap in the bending tree limbs, and red-eyed bats flutter low, dipping into the water for a fast drink, then soaring to meet the darkness.

The eerie sounds made Becka Munroe's skin tingle. She sat alert in the slender rowboat, every muscle in her body tensed and tight. She kept her eyes on the dark shoreline. Her hands on the oars felt cold and wet.

"Donny, you're crazy," she said, her voice muffled in the steamy night air. "I don't like this. We shouldn't be here."

"They won't miss their stupid rowboat," her boyfriend, Donny Albert, said. His oars splashed water, then hit sand. The river was shallow enough here for their boat to get stuck. "We'll leave it for them up on the shore."

"I'm not talking about stealing this boat," Becka said, fighting the shivers that rolled down her back despite the heat of the night. "Why are we here? Why are we on the river at night in this frightening swamp? I . . . I can't see a thing. There isn't even a moon."

Donny snickered. "For thrills," he said. "Life is so boring, Becka. Tenth grade is so boring. Go to school. Do your homework. Sleep and go to school again. We have to do something crazy. Something exciting."

Becka sighed. "I can't believe I agreed to come out here at night. Why did I do it?"

She could see his grin even in the dim light. "Because you're crazy about me?"

"Just plain crazy," she muttered.

Something splashed up from the water and thumped the side of the boat. "Did you hear that?" Becka cried. "What was it? A frog?"

"Snake, maybe," Donny said. "The river is crawling with them. Some are a mile long."

"Shut up!" Becka snapped. She had a sudden urge to take an oar and swing it at Donny's head. "You're not funny. It's scary enough out here without you trying to scare me more."

He laughed. "You're too easy to scare. It's not much of a challenge. I don't think —"

He didn't finish his sentence. His mouth remained open and his dark eyes bulged. He was staring past Becka. His chin began to quiver and

4

a low moan escaped his throat. He raised a finger and pointed.

Becka heard the splash of water behind her. And the heavy *slap* of footsteps on wet sand. "Donny — what?" she uttered. Then she turned and saw the huge creature.

It took her eyes a few seconds to focus. At first, she thought she was staring at a tall swamp bush, some kind of piney shrub looming up from the sandy bottom.

But as soon as she realized it was moving in the water, taking long, wet, splashing strides . . . she knew it was alive. Knew it was a terrifying creature.

"Row! Hurry! Row!" Donny's scream came out high and shrill. He bent over the oars and began to pull frantically. She could hear his wheezing breaths. But they were quickly drowned out by the grunts of the swamp monster that staggered toward them and its thudding, wet footsteps.

The creature stood at least ten feet tall. It was shaped like a human but covered in dark fur like a bear. Chunks of wet sand fell off its fur as it staggered forward. It raised its curled claws and uttered an angry howl of attack.

"Oh, help. Oh, help." One oar slipped out of Becka's hand. She grabbed at it and caught it before it dropped into the water. Then she leaned forward and began to row as hard as she could.

"Row faster!" Donny cried. "Faster! We can get away. It's slow. We can get —"

A hard jolt shook them both. Their bodies snapped forward, then back. The oars flew from Donny's hands.

Becka knew at once what had happened. The boat had hit a sandbar.

The swamp creature uttered another animal cry, like a bleating elephant. Water splashed high as it leaned forward and brought its clawed paws down, preparing to grab them.

His oars in the water, Donny rocked the boat from side to side. Becka desperately dug her oars into the sand, pulling . . . pulling.

With its prow stuck deep in the sloping sand hill, the boat didn't move. The two teenagers sat helpless as the grunting, howling creature advanced.

And as it loomed over them, spreading its arms, gnashing its pointed teeth, their final screams echoed off the bent trees, sending bats fluttering to the sky.

"What are you doing? Turn that off!"

Kelli Andersen jumped at the sound of her father's voice.

She watched him stride across the den, grab the remote, and click off the TV. He turned and squinted through his black-framed eyeglasses at Kelli and her brother, Shawn. They sat on the edges of the long black leather couch, a bowl of nacho chips between them.

Kelli crossed her arms in front of her and glared at him. "Why did you turn it off at the good part?" she demanded.

"Why were you watching that movie?" he asked. "*Swamp Beast III*?"

Shawn had his hands clasped tightly in his lap. His dark eyes were wide, his expression frightened. "Kelli wanted to show me where you're making us move to," he whispered.

Their dad shook his head. "By watching a horror movie?" He took off his glasses and rubbed the top of his nose. He did that a lot. It either meant he was thinking hard or he was trying to control his temper.

"Kelli, you're twelve," he said. "You're the older sister. You should know better."

"But, Dad —" Kelli started.

He raised a hand. "Silence. You know your brother is afraid of scary movies. You know Shawn has nightmares. How could you be so thoughtless?"

Kelli shrugged. "I . . . didn't think it would be that scary."

Of course that was a lame reply, but it was the best she could do. Kelli knew the truth. She really *did* want to scare Shawn. If he was seriously scared, maybe their dad wouldn't drag them away from New York City to a Florida swamp.

Shawn did that thing with his shoulders that he always did when he was feeling tense or scared. He kind of rolled them so that it looked like he was shivering. "Dad . . . ?" he started in a tiny voice. "Are there really swamp monsters where we are moving?"

Kelli groaned.

Their dad's cheeks reddened. He was totally bald, and when he got angry, the top of his head turned red, too. Kelli always thought he looked like a light bulb lighting up. A light bulb with glasses.

"Of *course* there aren't any swamp monsters," he told Shawn. He turned to Kelli. "Look how you scared Shawn. You should apologize to him."

"Sorry, Shawn," she finally muttered. "Sorry you got scared by a dumb movie."

"That's not much of an apology," her dad said. "*You* get scared sometimes, don't you, Kelli?"

"No," she answered. "I don't. Never."

Shawn suddenly shot his head forward and screamed, "BOO!" practically in Kelli's ear. He laughed. "Made you jump."

"Did not," Kelli said. "You can't scare me, wimpo."

"Hey, what have we said about calling names?" their dad demanded. He didn't wait for an answer. "Listen, you two. Living next to Deep Hole Swamp is going to be the most exciting year of your lives."

"Maybe *too* exciting," Kelli said. She tossed back her black hair. She knew she was about to cause trouble. About to frighten Shawn and annoy her father even more. But she didn't really care. *Whatever works*, she thought. *Whatever it takes to keep me in New York City with my friends.*

Her dad took the bait. "What do you mean by that, Kelli?"

"I went online," she said. "I read stuff about Deep Hole Swamp. A lot of people say there are

9

monsters living in the swamp. Just like in *Swamp Beast III*."

"Really?" Shawn asked in a tiny voice. He did his shoulder thing again.

"No. Not really," their father said, frowning at Kelli. "You know there's a lot of bad information online. You don't trust everything you read — do you?"

Kelli's dark eyes challenged her father. "Some things are true."

"Well, monster stories aren't true," he said. "I'm a scientist, remember?"

Kelli rolled her eyes. "We know. We know, Dr. Andersen. You're a marine biologist. You remind us every day."

Her dad gritted his teeth. Kelli knew she was making him angry. But she didn't care. She really didn't want to move to a swamp in Florida for a year.

After their parents divorced, their mom moved to Seattle. Kelli didn't want to live there, either. She only wanted to live in New York. Now she was going to have to split her time between TWO places she hated.

She saw Shawn, skinny, pale Shawn, sitting on the edge of the couch, trembling. She felt bad that she had to scare him. But what choice did she have?

"Shawn, what are you thinking?" their father asked. "I can see your brain spinning."

10

"Well . . ." Shawn hesitated. "If we get down to Florida . . . and we *do* see a swamp monster, Dad . . . can we come back home right away?"

Their father scowled at Kelli. "I'm warning you. Don't scare your brother again."

Kelli stuck out her chin. "You didn't answer Shawn's question, Dad."

He rubbed his bald head. "Tell you what. If we see a swamp monster, we'll invite it over for dinner."

3

On their first day of school in Florida, Kelli and Shawn stepped out of their house a little before eight o'clock. The sun was already high over the trees, and the air felt steamy and hot.

Their new house was a simple, square cottage at the end of a narrow road called Mangrove Street. There were four or five other similar cottages along the road. Mangrove Street led to the small town. But to walk to their school, they had to follow a twisting dirt path through the trees.

"I can't believe we're going to a school that isn't even on a street," Shawn complained. He kept adjusting the backpack on his back. He'd felt totally tense since waking up. In fact, he hadn't been able to sleep for most of the night.

He couldn't shut out the drone of the tree frogs and insects outside his bedroom window. But that wasn't what kept him awake. It was thinking about starting a new school in such a strange place that made him toss and turn all night.

"Swan Middle School," he muttered, hurrying to stay up with Kelli, who always walked fast. "Stupid name. They should call it *Swamp* Middle School."

"Stop muttering to yourself," Kelli said, swinging her arms as she walked. She'd seen power walkers do that on TV, and she'd swung her arms, taking long strides, ever since. "Why are you such a wreck, Shawn? You changed your clothes three times."

He didn't answer. "It's so hot," he said. "I'm sweating already. My armpits are all sticky."

"Thanks for sharing," Kelli said.

She stopped. The path cut through thick shrubs and rows of pale, smooth-barked trees. Large patches of the path were overrun by creeping grass and dried brown vines.

"Shawn — stop." She pointed. The vine tendril a few feet up ahead seemed to be moving.

"S-snake," Shawn stammered.

In a slender beam of sunlight, the snake appeared to glow. Silvery and long. It coiled and uncoiled itself as it slid silently across the path.

"Dad bought us that book about identifying snakes," Kelli said. "But I forgot to look at it."

Shawn glanced all around. "Probably thousands of snakes here. And a lot of them are poisonous."

"You mean venomous."

Shawn shuddered. "Remember that movie about the anaconda you made me watch last month?"

"Shut up," Kelli said. "I didn't make you watch it. You wanted to watch it."

"Did not. Think there are anacondas down here?"

"Probably," Kelli said.

Shawn stepped over a clump of grass and started to walk along the center of the path, eyes on the ground. Kelli rushed up behind him and pinched his arm really hard. "Snakebite!"

He screamed.

She laughed. "You really are a wimp."

"And you're mean," he muttered.

A few minutes later, the trees ended. Their school came into view past a grassy clearing.

"Is that the whole school?" Shawn cried. "It . . . it looks like two log cabins shoved together."

Kelli had her phone out. She was trying to get a signal. "I have to send a picture to Marci back home. She won't believe this place. It's like pioneer days or something."

She clicked a photo. Then she lowered her phone. "Hey, look. What are all those people doing?"

Kelli and Shawn trotted over the grass toward the back of the school. Kelli's new sneakers squeaked on the damp grass as she ran.

As they got closer, the crowd came into focus. Kids in shorts and T-shirts. Adults — probably teachers — huddled together beside the kids. They all seemed to be staring down at the ground.

"This is way weird," Shawn muttered.

Then they both saw the black-and-white patrol car with its light flashing red on its roof. And two officers in black — black shirts and shorts — at the front of the line of kids and teachers. The cops were bent over, staring down, studying something on the ground.

"Probably someone lost a contact lens," Kelli joked.

"And the police came to help look for it?" Shawn said. "I don't think so."

They stepped up to the edge of the crowd. No one looked up to greet them. No one spoke. The two cops muttered to each other. The only other sound was the chirp of crickets from the trees.

Kelli uttered a startled cry when she saw what everyone was staring at. Were they really footprints? Yes. Enormous footprints dug deep in the muddy ground.

Kelli stepped up beside a teacher. Her eyes followed the line of footprints. They led to the side of the school. The deep ruts in the ground were round, as big as pies. *Like elephant footprints*, Kelli thought. *But bigger.*

One policeman, down on his knees, smoothed a hand over one of the prints.

Shawn bumped up beside Kelli. "What kind of animal made those footprints?" He tried to whisper, but his voice carried in the silence. A few kids turned to stare at him.

Kelli shrugged. "Beats me."

A boy turned and strode up to Kelli and Shawn. He had a pale, round baby face topped by wavy white-blond hair. His blue eyes were round and bright. He had freckles on his cheeks.

"Want to know why everyone is scared?" he asked in a whisper. "The Shaggedy was here."

4

"Excuse me?" Kelli squinted at the kid. She studied him. With that perfect light blond hair and freckled, round face, he didn't look real. He reminded her of a doll she once had.

He wore baggy brown cargo shorts and a white T-shirt with an upside-down smiley face on the front. He was kind of chubby. His bare arms were pale and flabby. His hands were curled into tight fists.

"The Shaggedy," he repeated.

Kelli frowned at him. "Are we supposed to know what that is?" she said.

She realized he was studying her. "You're the new kids from New York?" he asked. There was something unpleasant in the way he said it, Kelli thought. The boy made a face like he had just smelled something bad.

Shawn's eyes were wide. "What's the Shaggedy?" he asked the boy.

17

"It lives in the swamp," the boy whispered. He glanced around quickly, as if he was telling a secret, as if he shouldn't be explaining this to them. "Under the water."

Shawn's mouth dropped open. Kelli put a hand on her brother's shoulder. "He's making this up," she whispered in his ear.

"No, I'm not," the boy insisted. He ran a chubby hand through his light blond hair. His blue eyes flashed excitedly. "The Shaggedy was here. Sometimes it gets restless. It climbs out of the swamp and it walks . . . It walks and it —"

A young woman interrupted, stepping between Kelli and Shawn and the boy. She had brown hair tied in a ponytail, dark eyes, and a nice smile. She had a small rhinestone in the side of her nose. She wore a pale blue T-shirt over a short black skirt.

"Don't listen to Zeke," she told Kelli and Shawn. "I'm Miss Rawls. I'm going to be your teacher. Don't listen to Zeke's stories." She patted him on the head. "He's got monsters on the brain."

Zeke rolled his eyes but didn't say anything.

"Was he telling you about a swamp monster?" Miss Rawls asked. "Let me assure you, there is no swamp monster."

Zeke pointed down at the footprints. "Check those out," he said. "Those aren't rabbit prints."

Miss Rawls shook her head. "This is someone's idea of a practical joke," she said. She narrowed

18

her eyes at Zeke. "Maybe you and your brother, Decker, made these footprints last night. I wouldn't be surprised."

Zeke took a step back. "No way!" he cried. "Decker and I . . . we don't go out at night. We know the Shaggedy is real."

"As real as the Easter Bunny," Miss Rawls said. She swatted a mosquito on her neck. "There's been a lot of rain," she told Kelli and Shawn. "It's insect heaven down here. Did you know that the mosquito is the state bird of Florida?"

Shawn and Kelli laughed. Kelli liked Miss Rawls already. *Her sense of humor is a lot like mine*, she thought.

Zeke scowled and stared down at one of the big muddy footprints. "Teachers don't know everything," he muttered. "Why do you think the police are here? *They* don't think it's a practical joke."

One of the policemen walked over to Miss Rawls. He was tall and thin, except for a belly that stretched the front of his shirt. He had a shaved head, squinty green eyes, and a scar across his chin. He wiped his sweaty forehead with one sleeve.

"I heard what y'all were saying," he said. He had a Southern accent. *Definitely not a New Yorker*, Kelli thought. "This isn't a joke. We think whoever — or whatever — made these

19

prints smashed a bunch of windows around the side of the building."

"Oh, that's terrible," Miss Rawls said, shaking her head.

"And the soccer goals out on the field are totally smashed," the policeman continued. He scratched his shaved head. "My partner and I started to follow the prints away from the school. They lead right back to the swamp."

Zeke pumped a fist in the air. "I told you so."

Kelli turned. Something caught her eye. Squinting into the bright morning sunlight, she saw a man, half-hidden behind a tree at the edge of the grass. A white-haired man in a floppy tan hat. He had a scraggly white beard and wore a safari jacket and khaki shorts. Hugging the tree, he stood watching everyone. He didn't move. He watched from a distance.

"Miss Rawls? Who is that?" Kelli asked, pointing.

But when she turned back, the man had vanished.

"I've got to get everyone inside," Miss Rawls said. "Enough excitement for one morning. School has to start sometime!" She motioned for Kelli and Shawn to follow her. "I'll introduce you two when class begins. We don't divide up into grades here," she explained. "The school is too small. Everyone is all together. That will

20

probably be hard for you to get used to. But you may learn to like it."

Kelli started to follow the teacher, but Shawn held back. She saw that his legs were trembling. His dark eyes seemed to be pleading with her.

"Tell me it isn't real," he said. "Tell me there's no such thing as a Shaggedy, that we didn't see footprints from a swamp monster on our very first morning. Please. Tell me."

Before Kelli could answer, Zeke put his hands on Shawn's shoulders and brought his face close to Shawn's. "Know how I know the Shaggedy is real?" Zeke said. "Because I saw him. Decker and I saw him, plain as day."

5

"I've been texting Marci," Kelli said. "She can't believe that all the grades are in one room."

"I can't believe it, either," Shawn said. "I'm sitting next to a first grader. Am I supposed to wipe his nose and sound out the words in his baby book to him?"

Kelli sighed. "I'm stuck in a swamp school with a bunch of hicks, and Marci is going to a Taylor Swift concert at Madison Square Garden tonight."

They were heading to lunch, which was in the next building. Kelli could smell the food as she pulled open the door and followed Shawn in. It actually smelled a lot like the cafeteria back at P.S. 87. Kelli saw a kitchen and food counter along one side. Wooden picnic tables filled the rest of the room.

She and Shawn grabbed a couple of ham sandwiches and bags of chips and turned with their trays to survey the room. The tables were filled with kids laughing and eating, voices ringing off the wooden walls and low ceiling.

"It doesn't matter where we sit," Kelli said. "We don't know anybody."

The only two places appeared to be across the table from Zeke. He had a big glop of something on his plate that might have been mashed potatoes and gravy. A drip of gravy had slid onto his chin. He slurped down the milk from a small milk carton, then opened another.

"Hey, Zeke. How's it going?" Kelli said, trying to be cheerful.

He burped.

Kelli and Shawn pulled out chairs and sat down. Shawn began tearing the Saran wrap off his sandwich. Kelli texted Marci:

LUNCH WITH MY LITTLE BRO. THRILLS, HUH?

She realized Zeke was staring at her phone. "You have your own phone?" he said, wiping his hands on the legs of his shorts. "Can I see it?" He grabbed it out of her hand.

"Hey —" Kelli reached to take it back.

Zeke raised it to his face, studying the screen. "What are all these little pictures?" he asked.

"You don't have a phone?" Kelli said. "Your parents won't let you?"

Zeke poked the screen several times. "No. My family never had a phone. My dad says he doesn't know anyone he wants to talk to."

"Well, how do you get texts or e-mails?" Shawn asked him. "How do you check Instagram?"

He handed the phone back to Kelli. She wiped gravy off the screen. "Instagram? Why would I want that?" He shook a fist at Shawn. "I have InstaFist."

Shawn laughed. But he stopped quickly when he saw Zeke's expression change. Zeke's blue eyes flashed angrily. "Don't laugh at me. Just because we're not New Yorkers . . . it doesn't mean we're stupid."

"Whoa. No way," Shawn said. "I didn't mean —"

Zeke stared at him for another long moment, then returned to his potatoes and gravy.

Kelli tried her sandwich, but it was dry and tasted like cardboard. Kids at the next table were tossing an apple up to the ceiling, catching it, tossing it again. They were laughing and shoving each other, trying to make the catcher miss.

She knew the conversation with Zeke wasn't going well. She decided to try one more time. "You know, Shawn and I aren't snobs. But it's been hard for us to leave our school and our friends and move so far away."

Zeke swallowed a lump of gravy. "Then why don't you go back? You don't belong here." He leaned over the table, challenging her. "When is the last time you went fishing?"

Kelli choked down a dry chunk of ham. "Fishing? You mean like in a boat? Never."

Zeke tossed his head back and laughed. "See what I mean? Never? Never been fishing? And you think you're so great?"

"I never said I was great," Kelli snapped back.

Zeke had a big smirk on his face. "Have you ever *been* in a boat?"

"A sailboat," Kelli answered. "My cousin goes sailing off Montauk on Long Island."

"Sailboat?" Zeke laughed again, shaking his head. "You don't belong here. Really. You'll *die* in this swamp."

Shawn made a gulping sound. He had been silent this whole time. But Zeke's words appeared to wake him up. He peered across the table at Zeke. "Did you really see the Shaggedy?" Shawn asked. "Did you really see a swamp monster? Or were you just trying to scare us?"

Zeke's smile faded. "You *should* be scared," he said, lowering his voice. "You saw those footprints outside. They weren't fake. I wasn't lying. Decker and I saw the Shaggedy. We saw it close up."

Shawn's mouth dropped open. He raised his hands to the sides of his face. "I . . ." He started to talk, but no sound came out.

Kelli put a hand on his shoulder. "Don't listen to him, Shawn. You've got to stop scaring yourself. You heard what Miss Rawls said about those footprints."

Zeke bent over and fumbled through his backpack. He pulled up a sheet of white paper. "Check

25

this out." He turned it around so Kelli and Shawn could see it.

Kelli squinted at it. A pencil drawing of a tall, hulking, half-human monster with slime dripping off its body.

"I drew this last week," Zeke said.

Kelli laughed. "Who *is* that? Cookie Monster from *Sesame Street*?"

Zeke growled. He slammed the drawing onto the table. His freckled cheeks darkened to red. "I warned you before," he muttered through gritted teeth. "Don't laugh at me."

Kelli felt a chill roll down her back. *He's unbalanced*, she thought. *This guy is seriously weird.*

A kid bumped up behind Zeke — *his exact double!*

Same round baby face, same blue eyes and short light-blond hair. Dressed in a red-and-white Florida State Seminoles T-shirt and red shorts that came down below his knees.

"Hey, this is my brother, Decker," Zeke said.

Decker scraped the chair next to Zeke away from the table and dropped down heavily beside his twin. "Yo," he muttered.

"This is Kelli and that's Shawn," Zeke said, motioning with his head. "They're from New York. He's okay, but she makes a lot of jokes."

Decker studied Kelli. "We don't think jokes are funny," he said. His voice was deeper than Zeke's.

"He was asking about the Shaggedy," Zeke said, waving his drawing in Shawn's direction.

"You think that's a joke, too?" Decker demanded.

Decker just sat down and he's already looking for a fight, Kelli thought.

"The Shaggedy isn't funny," Decker said, staring angrily at Kelli. "When he gets restless and climbs out of the swamp like last night, he can do very bad things. He wrecks everything in sight, and he hurts people."

"Sounds like a comic book I read," Kelli said.

Zeke tossed his spoon at her. She dodged to the side. It missed and clattered to the floor. "You should listen to Decker and me," he said. "New Yorkers don't know everything."

Decker laughed as if his brother had made a great joke. He had the same cold laugh as Zeke.

"They don't know *anything*," Zeke told Decker. "They've never even been fishing."

"Seriously?" Decker said, shaking his head. He leaned over and pulled up a tin can from his backpack. It was about the size of a coffee can. He reached two fingers into the can and pulled up a long, fat, purple worm. "Ever see one of these?"

He dangled the worm in front of Kelli's face. It glistened in the bright cafeteria light.

"Whoa. It's huge!" Shawn exclaimed.

Kelli narrowed her eyes at Decker. "Are you kidding me? You brought a worm to school?"

27

He nodded. "It's bait." He swung it at her. One end of the worm slapped her forehead. It felt warm and wet.

Kelli snapped her head back. She wiped worm slime off her skin.

Decker and Zeke both laughed. Then Decker swung the worm back toward his face. He lowered it slowly — and bit a big chunk off one end.

Kelli felt her stomach lurch. Shawn groaned. She watched Decker chew the worm. "Ewwww. Why'd you *do* that?" she gasped.

He swallowed the worm piece. "You want a taste?" He shot his hand forward and smeared the worm over Kelli's face, rubbing it into her forehead and cheeks.

Then the two brothers jumped up and trotted away, bumping knuckles and laughing the same laugh.

"Nice guys," Shawn muttered.

"I don't think I'm going to like it here," Kelli said.

Kelli was perched on the arm of the living room couch, phone pressed to her ear, deep in conversation with Marci in New York, when she heard Shawn's scream.

Her dad jumped up from behind his laptop on the dining room table.

"Tarantula!" Shawn screamed. "Help! It's got me!"

Tarantula?

The phone slid out of Kelli's hand and bounced onto the couch cushion. She saw Shawn across the room, frantically swatting at the front of his T-shirt.

"It's going to bite! It's going to bite!" he screamed.

Dad darted across the narrow, cluttered room and took Shawn's T-shirt in both hands. He gazed down at the round, dark creature stuck in the fabric.

"Help! Help me!" Shawn wouldn't stop scream-ing, his face twisted in panic.

"Not a tarantula," their dad reported calmly. "Shawn, calm down. It's a common American house spider."

Shawn made a choking sound. "What's the dif-ference? It's as big as a tarantula!"

Their dad plucked the spider off the shirt and carried it out the front door. "There are no taran-tulas down here," he said when he returned. "That's one thing you don't have to worry about."

Shawn rolled his eyes. He was still breathing hard. He brushed off the front of his T-shirt with both hands. "This place is *crawling* with insects."

"Why don't you start an insect diary, Shawn?" their dad suggested. "Keep a list and a descrip-tion of all the insects you find."

"For sure, Dad," Shawn muttered. "I'll get right on that."

Their father turned his gaze on Kelli, standing beside the couch, about to redial Marci. "You two should take advantage of living near a swamp," he told them. "It's a unique opportunity most kids will never have."

Kelli frowned at him. "Poor kids," she said. "Maybe someone would like to take my place?"

Their dad mopped sweat off his forehead with one hand. "I'm ignoring that, Kelli. This year will definitely help you get over your fear of insects, Shawn."

"What about *my* fear of never seeing my friends again?" Kelli said.

"That's why I bought you both cell phones. So you can talk to your friends whenever you want. There's even Wi-Fi down here." He pulled off his glasses and pinched the bridge of his nose. "You both promised to give it a try and not complain."

"That was before I saw this place," Shawn said. "Besides, when I promised, I had my fingers crossed."

"Dad," Kelli started, "you have to admit that dragging us to a swamp —"

He didn't let her finish. "Is a fabulous opportunity. And for me, it's a chance to solve the mysteries of the most mysterious swamp in Florida."

Kelli dropped onto the couch with a sigh. "I don't want to complain, Dad. Really. But you should see our school. It's so small. It looks like someone's garage."

"And the kids are totally weird," Shawn added. "These two kids — Zeke and Decker . . . They're, like, from a horror movie."

"They are these blond twins with scary blue eyes," Kelli said. "One of them ate a fat worm at lunch."

Her dad chuckled. "That's good protein."

"Not funny, Dad," Shawn said. "They keep trying to scare us. They say they've seen this swamp monster called the Shaggedy."

31

Their dad blinked. Kelli could see him suddenly alert, thinking hard. "The Shaggedy," he muttered. "I've heard that legend."

"You've heard about it?" Shawn asked. "You mean, it's *real*?"

"Of *course* it's not real. I *said* it's a legend. It's a story that got passed down. That's all."

"But we saw the monster's footprints," Shawn said. "Behind the school."

"You're New Yorkers, remember? You don't fall for stuff like that."

"Zeke and Decker made fun of us because we're New Yorkers and we've never gone fishing," Kelli said.

Their father clapped his hands together. "Let's take care of that right now. Go to your rooms and change. I'm going to take you fishing on the river."

Kelli squinted at him. "Seriously?"

"Let's do it," he said, trying to force them to be enthusiastic. "Let's go. You'll enjoy it. And after today, those guys at school won't be able to accuse you of never doing it."

Kelli and Shawn hurried to their rooms. The rooms faced each other in the back of the little house. Kelli still hadn't gotten used to how small her room was. It was the size of her closet in their apartment back home.

"I don't know what to wear," Shawn called from across the hall. "What's wrong with what I'm wearing? Shorts and a T-shirt."

"Put on a long-sleeved shirt," Dad called. "To protect from insects."

"Insects? What kind of insects?" Shawn shouted.

Dad laughed. "Dont worry about it. Just change your shirt. I've got plenty of bug spray."

Shawn changed his shirt and made his way back to the living room. His father was holding a fishing rod in each hand. "Where did you get those?" Shawn asked.

"Bought them. And I bought a rowboat, too." He was about to say something else. But Kelli came bursting into the room, eyes wide, shouting. "Look at this! Hey — look at this!"

She shoved her yellow backpack toward her dad's face. "I don't believe this. Look what someone wrote."

All three of them stared at the bloodred words crudely scrawled on the front of the backpack:

HERE COMES THE SHAGGEDY!

"One of your new friends is playing jokes on you." Their dad chuckled.

"It isn't funny," Kelli insisted. "It's a brand-new backpack."

"Maybe it'll wash out."

Kelli frowned. "It had to be Zeke or Decker. Trying to be scary."

Shawn rubbed a finger over the scrawled red words. "Are you sure it's a joke? They said they don't like jokes."

"What *else* would it be?" Kelli snapped.

Her little brother's dark eyes locked on hers. "A warning?"

Kelli groaned. "Stop it, Shawn. Don't tell me this dumb prank is scaring you."

Shawn didn't reply.

A short while later, they were in a rowboat on the narrow, winding river that curled around the swamp. Sunlight made the water sparkle. Birds chattered in the smooth-trunked trees that leaned over the shore.

"Welcome to Deep Hole Swamp," their dad said. He sat in the prow with Shawn in the middle and Kelli behind Shawn. Kelli and Shawn practiced rowing while their father acted as tour guide. The fishing rods hung over the sides of the narrow boat.

"Is the water deep?" Shawn asked, peering over the side into the brown-green water.

"This part of the river is very shallow," Dad replied. He tugged his Mets baseball cap lower to shield his eyes from the sun. "You could climb out and walk, Shawn."

"Okay. I will," he said quickly. "I don't like boats."

Their dad shook his head. "I know sometime soon I'm going to find something you *do* like. Right now, the list of *don't likes* is very long."

"I don't like lists, either," Shawn said, finally smiling.

All three of them laughed.

"See that flowering plant over there?" their dad said, pointing. "That's very rare. It's called a scrub buckwheat. It's endangered. I'm excited to see it here."

"And what's that little plant with the white flowers over there?" Kelli asked. Living in an apartment in New York, she'd always wanted to plant some kind of garden but, of course, she didn't have a backyard where she could do it.

"That's called snakeroot," he said. "It's very rare, too. Some people think it's good for snakebite."

Shawn's eyes jumped at the sound of the word *snakebite*. He opened his mouth to say something, but changed his mind.

"You two aren't rowing together. You have to get in a rhythm," their father said.

Shadows from the trees on shore danced over the water. A light breeze didn't keep the air from becoming sticky and hot. A cyclone of tiny black insects buzzed to their left, thousands of them, rising high over the swamp. Kelli tilted her head up, enjoying the warmth of the sun on her face.

The river grew wider, and the current suddenly felt strong. "This is where the water starts to get deep," their father told them. "And over there is the outlet to the ocean."

"The river flows right into the Atlantic?" Kelli asked.

"Actually, the ocean flows into the river," he answered. "The river fills with salt water at that point. Ocean creatures find themselves swimming here."

"So . . . it gets really deep?" Shawn asked, peering over the side again. Rippling shadows from the water reflected on his face.

Their dad nodded. "No one knows how deep it is, because no one has ever reached the bottom. Some say it may be the deepest hole on earth."

"And that's why they call it Deep Hole Swamp," Kelli said.

"Duh," Shawn said.

"We have a whole year," Dad said. "I hope to explore every part of the swamp and then write a book about it."

Shawn stopped rowing. "And maybe you'll write about swamp monsters?" he asked.

"At least you're not obsessed," Kelli said to her brother, rolling her eyes.

"You're going to hear a lot of crazy stories about this swamp," their dad said, squinting into the distance. The rowboat slid through wide whirlpools, white against the green water.

"Some say the hole leads down to a chamber deep in the earth where monsters and strange sea creatures live," he continued. "Since no one has been able to dive to the bottom or send a camera that deep, no one can say for sure if anything at all can live down there."

Shawn stared down into the rippling water. "So maybe monsters . . ." he started.

His dad quickly cut him off. "Stories. All stories. All made-up," he said. "I'll say it again and again. You're not going to see any monsters down here. If Kelli hadn't shown you that stupid

37

movie, you wouldn't even be *thinking* about monsters."

Kelli rolled her eyes again. "I thought we were going fishing. I didn't know we were just going to get a lecture."

It took a while to get the fishing rods prepared. They fumbled in the tackle box, trying to figure out which hooks to use, then which bait to put on the hooks.

"Owww," Kelli said as her dad jammed a worm onto her hook. "Doesn't that hurt the worm?"

"Probably doesn't feel too good," her dad replied.

They practiced casting the line into the water. The small boat drifted with the current. The sun lowered, sending jagged sparkles of red over the flat waters.

It's really pretty here, Kelli thought. *You can't see colors like this in New York.*

And then she uttered a shout as something tugged the line. She raised the fishing rod, grabbed the reel. Something was pulling the line — fast.

"What do I do? What do I do?" Kelli cried.

"Reel it in," her dad said. "Hold the line tight. Pull back. Pull back. Reel it in."

Kelli tried to follow his instructions. But whatever had grabbed her line was big and strong. The rowboat rocked from side to side as she struggled with the line.

Shawn made a whimpering sound. He put down his fishing rod and grabbed the sides of the boat, holding on tightly as it rocked and bobbed.

The boat rocked harder as Kelli worked the line. The rod flew up and down, started to arch, and appeared about to bend in half as the creature fought to stay free.

"You're doing it!" her father yelled. "Keep working! You're bringing it in. It's something big. It —"

Kelli gave a hard yank. She screamed as an enormous creature came flying up from the water. Black and shiny, it quivered and flapped as it swung on the end of her line.

She cried out as the creature swung toward her — and hit her face with a loud *slaaaap*. The big, glistening thing spread itself over Kelli's face. Her hands flew up. The rod fell from her hands, into the river.

She stood in the rocking boat, grabbing at it. The boat heaved hard — and Kelli sailed over the side. She sent up a high wave as she splashed facedown into the green-brown water.

Sinking below the surface . . . the soupy, thick water rising over her . . . the water so thick and warm . . . the creature wrapping itself around her head.

I can't breathe, she realized. *It . . . it's SMOTHERING me.*

As Kelli struggled in the water, the creature pressed itself to her face. She could feel something pulsing inside it. Its heartbeat? Her chest felt about to explode.

Strong arms gripped her under the shoulders and pulled her up. As she rose to the surface, the creature slid off her face and disappeared, a large black spot swimming smoothly, wings outspread.

Her dad was standing in the water. He helped her lift herself into the rowboat. She sucked in breath after breath after he hoisted himself up after her.

Shawn hadn't moved. He gripped the sides of the boat so hard, his hands were white. He stared up at Kelli, his face frozen in fright.

"Wh-what was that?" Kelli finally managed to say. Her whole body shuddered. The sun wasn't warming her fast enough.

"I'm not sure," her dad answered. He turned to Shawn. "It wasn't a swamp monster. So don't say it."

Shawn shrugged. He didn't let go of the sides.

"It may have been an eagle ray," their dad continued. "They are very big manta rays. But they are ocean creatures. It must have gotten lost."

"It — it tried to smother me," Kelli stammered.

"I don't think so," her dad said. "I think it was as scared as you were. So it just held on to you."

He hugged her. "Wish I'd brought some towels."

"Well, we didn't plan to go swimming," Kelli said, shaking water from her hair. "Whoa. I can still feel that thing on my face. Thanks for jumping in, Dad."

"I tried to get to you as fast as I could." He hugged her again. "You were really frightened. But, remember, you don't have to be afraid of all the animals here. The influx of salt water brings interesting creatures into this swamp."

"Yeah. Interesting," Kelli repeated. She shivered. She gazed at Shawn. His hands still gripped the boat sides. He was trembling.

I'm as frightened as he is, now, Kelli thought. *I have a very bad feeling about this swamp. We have to get out of here.*

*   *   *

41

Art class, Kelli discovered, was held in a trailer outside the school grounds. There were eight sixth graders in her new school, and they all took art at the same time. Since the school had only three teachers, Miss Rawls was also the art teacher.

Kelli found everyone sitting around a long picnic table that stretched the length of the room. "There's a spot for you, Kelli," Miss Rawls said, pointing to an empty space on the bench across from Zeke and Decker. "Today is free drawing day. Draw whatever comes into your head."

"I've never had class in a trailer before," Kelli said, squeezing to the end of the bench.

"It's not a trailer. It's a mobile home," Miss Rawls said. "Cozy, right?"

Kelli dropped her backpack on the floor, then leaned over the table to see what Zeke and his twin were drawing. Monsters, naturally.

Miss Rawls had her eyes on their sketches, too. She shook her head. "You two are obsessed. What is your problem?"

"Our problem is, Decker and I saw the Shaggedy," Zeke answered, not looking up from his paper. "We saw it close up. No lie."

"Zeke, please —" Miss Rawls started.

But Zeke was determined to tell his story. "It climbed out of the swamp one night," he said.

Kelli laughed. She quickly realized she was the only one. The other kids had stopped drawing and were gazing solemnly at Zeke. Even Miss Rawls had stopped grinning at him.

"It climbed out of the swamp, dripping wet," Zeke continued, speaking in a low voice just above a whisper. "Decker and I watched it stagger around for a bit. Then it stomped down the main path and came up to our neighbors' house across the road."

"It left huge wet footprints on the ground," Decker added.

"It pounded on our neighbor's front door," Zeke said. "It pounded so hard, the whole house shook, and the door cracked."

"But no one was home," Decker said, twirling his black marker between his fingers. "The monster let out a roar. Like it was angry. It was like a tiger's roar. It picked up a garbage can and *heaved* it into the trees. Then I guess it gave up."

Zeke nodded. "Decker and I followed it back to the swamp. We stayed way back. We didn't want the huge creature to see us. We were way scared. But we followed it to the river, and we watched it swim away."

"We watched it till it disappeared under the water," Decker said.

Silence for a long moment. Then Miss Rawls said, "Good story, guys. You should save it for Creative Writing class."

Zeke raised his right hand. "I didn't make it up. I swear it's true."

Miss Rawls turned to Kelli. "Don't listen to these two storytellers. I told you, they're monster crazy. And they love scaring new students."

"It should be a movie," Kelli said.

Zeke and Decker both grinned. They seemed to like that answer.

Kelli took a charcoal pencil and began to sketch. She wanted to draw a rowboat on the river. She drew tall vines along the river's edge. And she put a dark spot in the water beside the boat. The mysterious sea creature she had pulled from the water.

She loved to draw. When she was younger, she liked to draw sketches of her neighborhood in New York, and she liked to draw dogs. She made up a lot of crazy breeds. One year, she took a summer art course and her instructor said she had talent.

Now, she couldn't get the river to look right. It was so hard to draw water.

The class ended before she could finish. She handed her sketch to Miss Rawls and followed the others out of the trailer.

It was a steamy, hot afternoon, the sun high in the sky. The air was heavy and wet. Kelli always felt as if she was walking underwater here.

She crossed the grass to the main school building and ducked inside. The bright sunlight lingered in her eyes. When they finally adjusted to the dimmer light, she saw her brother at the end of the hall. He was standing stiffly at his locker. The locker door was open.

Something about the way he was standing, not moving at all, made Kelli realize something was wrong. "Hey, Shawn!" she called to him as she trotted toward him.

She stopped a few feet away. "Shawn? What happened? Who did this?"

She stared at the dark pond of water spread on the floor in front of the locker. Then she saw that the inside of the locker was wet, too, with bits of weeds clinging to the locker walls.

Shawn stared at her wide-eyed, his mouth hanging open.

"Shawn? Are you okay?" she cried.

"When I opened my locker . . ." he said finally, in a trembling voice. "When I opened my locker, everything was wet. My books . . . Kelli, look at my books. They're all soaked."

"Oh, wow," Kelli muttered, shaking her head. "Wow."

"And look," Shawn said. "Look at this." He shoved a folded-up sheet of paper into her hand. "This was stuffed in my locker."

"What is it?" Kelli asked. She unfolded the sheet of paper and saw that it was a note. She blinked as she read the words, scribbled in red ink:

THE SHAGGEDY WANTS YOU NEXT, SHAWN.

"We have to make those idiot twins stop this," Kelli said. She and Shawn walked out the back entrance and crossed the wide patch of grass behind the school. "They're obsessed with monsters. They ruined all your books for their stupid joke."

"But what if it's not a joke?" Shawn asked, hurrying to keep up with Kelli's long strides. What if it's real?"

Kelli didn't answer his question. "Wait till Dad hears about this," she said, swinging her fists as she walked.

Some kids were tossing a red Frisbee back and forth across the grass. At the hoop hung on the side of the school, six or seven girls had started a basketball game.

Wish I had time for fun, Kelli thought. *Wish there was someone here who I could be friends with.*

She hadn't heard from Marci in New York for a whole day. Was Marci forgetting about her?

They reached the line of trees. Several dirt paths led through the woods here. "I . . . don't remember which path to take to get home," Shawn said.

"Follow me," Kelli told him. "It's easy. Remember? Dad said to turn left at the sixth cypress tree, and we'll be on the right path."

"Didn't he say to turn right?"

"No. Left," Kelli said. "If we turn right, we'll end up back at school."

Shawn nodded, but he still looked doubtful.

"Here we are," Kelli said. She took him by the shoulders and led him onto the path. "This will take us home."

"It doesn't look like the one we walked this morning," Shawn said, gazing from tree to tree.

"That's because we were heading in the other direction," Kelli replied.

They walked for a while. Insects hummed over their head. Kelli and Shawn stopped when they saw a thin, pale green snake wriggle across the path. The trees along both sides of the path formed a thick, tangled fence. They fluttered in a light breeze, but the breeze didn't cool anything off.

"So hot here," Shawn muttered.

The path curved sharply to the left. They had to step over prickly vine tendrils. Above them, the sky darkened as low clouds suddenly covered the sun.

"Who turned off the lights?" Shawn joked.

47

Kelli glanced up. The sky was charcoal gray now. The clouds slid rapidly, bumping together, growing even darker.

Kelli stopped. Shawn stumbled into her. "Hey, what's wrong?"

The wind picked up. The tree limbs over their heads began to quiver and shake.

Kelli felt a drop of rain on her forehead. "I think this is the wrong path," she said. "I don't recognize anything, and we seem to be heading to the river."

Shawn made a gulping sound. "Wrong path? How can it be the wrong path?" he whined.

Kelli scrunched up her face, thinking hard. "Dad said turn left after the sixth cypress tree. But I think maybe I counted wrong."

"You *what*?"

"Shawn, you know I'm math-challenged."

"You couldn't count to *six*?" he cried. "You're not math-challenged. You're math-*stupid*!"

Kelli forced herself to stay calm. "It won't help to pick a fight. I admit I have a problem. I guess it's a phobia about math. When I count my fingers, I get eleven."

"That's because you're a mutant," Shawn muttered. "What are we going to do now? There's no one around to help us, and it's starting to rain."

"Stay calm," Kelli told him. "Don't panic."

"But what are we going to *do*?"

"Maybe we should backtrack," Kelli said. "Go

back the way we came and then find the path we're supposed to take."

Rain began to patter the ground. The rain slapping the fat vine leaves at their feet sounded like drumbeats all around them.

Shawn shook his head. He did his shoulder thing. "This is my worst nightmare," he said, talking to himself. "Lost in the middle of the swamp. All alone here, and it's starting to storm." His whole body shuddered.

"You're not all alone. I'm here," Kelli said.

He rolled his eyes. "You know what I meant."

"I know," she said. "Let's call Dad. He can direct us."

"Or come get us," Shawn said softly.

They both pulled out their phones. Kelli's heart was beating hard. She should have thought of calling him sooner. She raised the phone to her face. "Oh, wow," she moaned. "No bars."

"Me too," he said, shaking his head.

"There isn't any cell service in this swamp, Shawn." She slid the phone back into her pocket.

The sky was black as night now. Rain puddles began to form in the dirt path. The wind shook the trees all around them.

The trees next to Kelli let out sharp creaks. Their roots stretched way beyond their trunks. Roots that looked like legs, Kelli thought.

The wind gusted — and the trees moved.

They're walking! Kelli leaped back. No. It was just an illusion.

"Let's get out of here," she said.

Shawn wiped rainwater off his forehead. "Which way?" he asked, his voice tiny, muffled by the steady drumbeat of rain.

"Keep going, I guess," Kelli said. "We'll see what we come to."

Ducking their heads, they started along the path. A clap of thunder, like an explosion, made them jump.

Shawn gasped. Lightning crackled, and the vines and trees turned an eerie yellow-green in its glow. Kelli was taking long strides now, her arms crossed in front of her. She splashed through a puddle, kicking up mud as she walked.

Shawn struggled to keep up with her. He brushed raindrops from his eyes. It was so hard to see in the darkness.

Another crackle of lightning. A tree limb cracked ahead of them. It dropped onto the path. Another boom of thunder seemed to shake the trees.

Then the rain began to pour down harder. Sheets of rain, driven by fierce gusts of wind.

"I . . . I can barely see." Kelli tried to wipe the pounding water from her eyes.

Waves of rain pushed them back.

"I can't walk," Shawn cried, trying to press his way against the storm. "What are we going to *do*?"

10

Sheets of rain drove them back. The path disappeared under lakes of rainwater. Shawn said something, but Kelli couldn't hear him over the steady roar of rain.

Their shoes sank in mud now. They leaned into the howling wind and rain and struggled to move forward. "Dad must be worried about us," Kelli said.

"What? I can't hear you," came Shawn's faint reply.

The path curved sharply between two rows of slender-trunked trees. Shielding her eyes with one hand, Kelli squinted into the distance. And saw a cabin.

A square wooden cabin, half-hidden under the trees. The front window was dark. Rain cascaded off the slanted roof.

"Shawn — look!" she gasped, pointing.

He saw it, too. Without another word, they turned off the path and pushed their way through the narrow gaps between tree trunks. Kelli was breathing hard by the time she reached the small muddy clearing in front of the cabin.

Squinting against the rain, Kelli stared at the dark shack. The wooden walls were peeling. The door tilted on its hinges. A rusted metal rake lay upside down in the mud beside the door.

"Hey! Anyone home?" Kelli shouted. She and Shawn pounded on the front door. Lightning crackled behind them, followed by a ground-shaking boom of thunder.

Water rolled off the low roof like a waterfall and splashed on both sides of the cabin. "Hello? Anyone here?" Kelli shouted again. She backed up a step, peered into the dark window. Saw no signs of anyone moving.

A gust of wind swirled the rain into their faces. Kelli ducked her head. She grabbed the rusted doorknob — and tugged the cabin door open.

"Huh?" She uttered a short cry, startled that it opened so easily. The cabin was dark inside. Light from the open door washed over the front room.

Kelli poked her head in. The sour aroma of stale food greeted her nose.

"Hello? Hello?" Her voice bounced off the cabin walls.

"Move over," Shawn said. He bumped past her and stumbled inside. His whole body shuddered. "I'm totally soaked," he said. "I'll never get dry."

Kelli followed him into the cabin. It appeared to have only one room. Lightning flickered, lighting the room for a second or two.

Kelli glimpsed a small wooden table, a stove with a frying pan on it, a narrow sink.

And then her eyes stopped on the wall to their right. Shawn's gaze was already there.

They stared at the wall — and then they both began to scream.

11

"Skulls!" Shawn cried. "A whole wall of skulls!"

Lightning flashed outside, sending a spotlight over the wall and making the skulls appear to glow.

As her eyes adjusted, Kelli realized they were staring at rows of animal skulls, large and small. The skulls were lined up carefully in rows.

Shawn pointed with a trembling finger. "Those little ones . . . they're snake skulls. Look how many . . ." His voice trailed off.

"Whoever lives here must be some kind of hunter," Kelli said. She spun away from the wall of skulls, but she couldn't get the picture from her mind. *So many dead creatures.*

Hugging herself to try to warm up, she moved across the cabin. She stopped in front of a small wooden table. Several knives were lined up on the table. Kelli saw a large butcher knife and some smaller knives.

"This guy killed a lot of snakes," Shawn said behind her.

Thunder shook the cabin. Kelli saw a single shriveled strip of burned bacon in the frying pan on the stove. An unwashed dinner plate sat in the sink. A low shelf held a row of dusty glass jars.

Kelli squinted at the jar on the end. *Those are olives,* she told herself. *They CAN'T be eyeballs. Can they?*

"I . . . I don't like this," Shawn stammered. He was still staring at the skulls on the wall. He turned to Kelli. "Remember in *Swamp Beast III*? There was that creepy guy, the swamp hermit? Remember? He lived by himself in a cabin just like this, and he was totally insane?"

"I remember," Kelli said. "Shawn, don't get yourself all worked up."

"He had some kind of crazy mind control over snakes," Shawn continued, ignoring her. "And he kept sending the snakes out to strangle people in their sleep. And — and —"

"Shut up, Shawn!" Kelli cried. "You're scaring yourself to death. That was only a movie. There's no such thing as a swamp hermit," she said — and the cabin door swung open.

They turned and watched a man step inside. He wore a long trench coat and a wide-brimmed hat drenched from the rain.

When he pulled the hat off, Kelli saw his white, scraggly beard.

She recognized him. The man she'd seen hiding behind a tree on their first morning at school. The morning of the huge footprints in the ground. This was the man who stood still as a statue and watched the whole thing from a distance.

Kelli and Shawn froze, staring at him.

He started to pull off his trench coat, but stopped when he spotted them. A thin smile formed under the white beard. "Why, hello," he said in a hoarse, scratchy voice. "Do I have visitors?"

He turned and carefully latched the cabin door.

12

He just locked us in, Kelli realized.

She watched the man slide off his trench coat and hang it on a hook by the door. He slung his big rain hat over the coat. He tugged at his white ponytail, squeezing rainwater out. Then he turned back to them with that same thin smile on his bearded face.

Kelli studied his eyes. They were silver-gray — cold eyes a color she'd never seen on a person before. He had deep ruts down both of his cheeks. His skin appeared leathery, lined with tiny cracks, as if he'd spent too much time in the sun.

He took a few steps toward them, adjusting his red-and-black-checked flannel shirt over his baggy khaki shorts. The cabin floorboards squeaked under his shoes.

"I — I'm sorry we barged in here like this," Kelli stammered. "I'm Kelli and this is my brother, Shawn. We . . . just wanted to get out of the rain."

57

"We were lost," Shawn added. "We took the wrong path."

The man's cold gray eyes studied them both. "You shouldn't wander in the swamp," he said. "There are so many dangerous creatures."

Like swamp hermits? Kelli thought.

"Well, your front door just opened," Kelli said, her heart pounding. "We didn't mean to break in. We didn't know how else to get dry. But we're sorry if we —"

He waved a hand to silence her. "No worries," he said softly.

Lightning flashed outside. The crackle sent a chill down Kelli's back.

We're locked in.

The man crossed the room, the thin smile frozen on his face. "Your father is the scientist?" he asked.

"Yes," they both answered at once. "He's probably out looking for us," Kelli added quickly. "Do you know our dad?"

The eerie silver eyes locked on Kelli. "I try to know everyone," the man said.

"Well, we'll get going," Kelli said, inching toward the door. "If you tell us how to get to the right path . . ."

"I'm Ranger Saul," the man said, ignoring her. "I used to work for the Park Service," he said. "I know every inch of Deep Hole Swamp. But I don't work for the Park Service anymore. They fired me." He lowered his eyes. "I don't want to talk about why."

Shawn brought his face up close to Kelli's. "He's scary," Shawn whispered.

Kelli nodded. She had her eyes on the cabin door. Could the two of them make it out the door before this guy Ranger Saul stopped them?

"I know the people, and I know the creatures of this swamp," Saul said. "I know the trees and the strange junglelike plants. I know plants down here that eat meat. Do you believe that?" His eyes challenged them.

"Meat-eating plants and creatures you don't find in the tourist guidebooks," he continued. He uttered a dry laugh that sounded more like a cough. "But I'm no longer a ranger. Not good enough for them, I guess. But why am I telling you this?"

He stepped up to the table holding the knives. He picked up the butcher knife and ran his finger down the blade. His cold, silvery eyes were on Kelli.

"Why am I telling you this?" he repeated, his voice growing shrill.

He raised the knife. He ran his finger slowly down the blade one more time. His eyes remained on Kelli.

"No!" she cried, raising her hands as if to shield herself. "No! Please — don't!"

13

Saul's eyes went wide. He jerked back, startled by her cry. He set the knife down on the table. "I'm so sorry," he said. "I was just inspecting the blade."

Kelli let out a sigh of relief. Her eyes went to the collection of skulls on the wall. "Are you a hunter?" she asked.

Saul nodded. He turned away from the knife table and crossed the room to the skulls. "Part of my job used to be animal control," he said. "I was very good at it."

He means he killed a lot of animals, Kelli thought.

Saul waved a hand at the wall. "These are some trophies," he said. "Animals I caught. See that one?" He wiped his hand over the top of the skull. "That's an anaconda."

"Wow," Shawn murmured. "A real one?"

Saul nodded. "As real as they get. It's a beauty, isn't it?" He didn't wait for them to answer. "I got into making things out of snakeskin," he continued. "You know. Wallets and things. Made some really nice-looking belts. And a pair of gloves."

He smoothed a hand over a few more skulls. "These beauties are some of the snakes who contributed their skins."

Kelli shivered. *Why would a park ranger love to kill snakes? Wasn't his job to* protect *them? And how weird was it to decorate a wall with snake heads? This man has to be totally twisted.*

Shawn glanced out the window. "Are there . . . are there lots of dangerous snakes out there?"

Saul swept a hand down his white beard. His silvery eyes grew wide. "The swamp is home to many snake species," he told Shawn. "You know about the pythons, don't you?"

Shawn gasped. "Huh? Pythons?"

Saul nodded.

He enjoys scaring us, Kelli thought.

"Some pet owners had pythons they didn't want to keep," Saul explained. "So they dumped them in the swamp. They didn't think about how snakes multiply and multiply. They didn't think about how these big, powerful snakes could take over a swamp."

Shawn shivered. "You mean . . . ?"

"There are hundreds of them in the swamp," Saul said. He leaned toward them and continued in a raspy whisper: *"Hundreds of deadly pythons!"*

Shawn's eyes were wide with fright. He had jammed his fists into his pants pockets and was suddenly breathing hard.

Kelli brought her face close to his. "This guy is creeping me out," she whispered. "Let's go."

They began inching their way to the door.

Saul moved quickly, stepping in front of them, blocking their path. "Don't hurry away," he said. "Aren't you going to stay until the rain stops?"

"We're late. Dad will be worried," Kelli said. "We'd better go."

"I want to warn you —" Saul started.

But Kelli didn't let him finish. She dove around him, pulling Shawn with her. And as Saul spun in surprise, she flipped open the latch, flung the door wide, and the two of them ran out into the rain.

The sky was still nearly as dark as night. Fat raindrops spattered her head and shoulders.

They both splashed up mud and waves of rain-water as they ran. Kelli's legs felt heavy, her heart raced in her chest, but she forced herself to move. Shawn uttered short gasps as he ran close behind her.

Kelli heard a sound. Glanced back. Was the strange, frightening man chasing after them?

Yes. Yes, he was.

His boots pounded the wet, muddy ground. His eerie eyes were wide. His scraggly white hair flew around his head as he ran.

We can't outrun him, Kelli thought. *He's going to catch us.*

She pictured the dozens of skulls lined up on his wall.

Yes, he's going to catch us.

And THEN what?

14

Kelli and Shawn turned to face him.

Saul came to a stop. Panting hard, he leaned forward, put his hands on his knees, and struggled to catch his breath.

"Why are you chasing us?" Kelli demanded.

He stood up, still breathing hard. "I just wanted to help you," he said. "Point you in the right direction. You said you were lost."

Kelli studied his face. Was he telling the truth? Did he just want to be helpful? Or was he trying to scare them?

Saul pointed. "That way. Just past those tall pine trees. That's the path you want. You can follow it to your house."

"Thank you," Kelli said.

"Be careful," Saul said. His eyes locked on hers. "Be *very* careful."

Kelli turned away, a chill at the back of her neck. She didn't like the man's stare. She didn't like the dark look in his eyes.

Was he giving them a friendly warning?

Or was it a threat?

"I think you should stay away from him," their dad said at dinner. "Sometimes strange people go off and live by themselves in the swamp."

"Swamp hermits," Shawn said. "We saw one in *Swamp Beast III*."

Dr. Andersen shook his head. "You can't get that movie out of your head, can you, Shawn?" He flashed a scowl at Kelli.

Kelli looked away and took a bite of her Sloppy Joe sandwich. That was her dad's specialty. Hamburger meat in a tangy sauce on a bun. He made Sloppy Joes once a week because he didn't know how to cook much of anything else.

Ever since the divorce, their dad said he'd had to learn a whole bunch of "Homemaking Skills." Cooking hadn't been one of them. Kelli found herself making dinner a lot of the time.

"The man called himself Ranger Saul," Kelli said. "Do you think he really was a park ranger?"

Her dad shrugged. "Hard to say. He could be telling the truth."

"He said they fired him," Shawn chimed in. "Probably because he's totally weird. I mean, a whole wall of snake skulls?"

"Weird," their dad repeated. "Yes, that qualifies as weird."

Kelli shuddered. "I know I'm going to dream about those skulls for weeks."

"I thought you were the brave one," her dad said, wiping the orange sauce off his chin.

"The whole thing was Kelli's fault," Shawn said. "If she could count trees, we wouldn't have gotten lost. But she can't even count to six."

"Don't make fun of your sister," their dad scolded. "You know she has a problem with numbers. You don't want her to make fun of *you*, do you?"

"And there's a *lot* I could make fun of," Kelli added. "Should I make a list?"

"Ha-ha." Shawn tossed a potato chip across the table at her. Kelli grabbed it and ate it.

"How old are you?" their father asked Shawn. "You're still throwing food?"

Shawn started to reply, but his expression suddenly changed. "I almost forgot," he said. He dug into his pants pocket and pulled out a folded-up sheet of paper.

"Would anyone like another sandwich?" their dad asked. "There's plenty left."

"Wait," Shawn said. "Don't get up, Dad. You have to see this. It's a note I found in my locker."

He took the note from Shawn and read it out loud: "*The Shaggedy wants you next, Shawn.*" He rubbed his bald head. "Someone is playing a joke here."

"My locker was filled with swamp water," Shawn said. "It wasn't funny. My books were all ruined. And this note was there."

Dad stared at the scrawled words, frowning. He handed the note back to Shawn. "I guess you're supposed to think this creature called a Shaggedy is going to come and get you. And drag you into the swamp or something. You're not really scared — are you?"

Shawn hesitated. "Well . . ."

"No reason to be scared," his dad said. "You know as well as I do, there's no such thing as a Shaggedy." Behind his glasses, his eyes twinkled. "Hey, why don't you play a trick on those two kids? Zeke and Decker? I'm sure we could think of something that's actually funny. They probably like jokes."

"I don't think so," Kelli chimed in. "I don't think that's a good idea. I wouldn't want to mess with these two guys. Seriously."

After dinner, Kelli texted a bunch of her friends back in New York. And she talked to Marci for nearly half an hour. "I'm so totally homesick," she told her friend. "It's like another planet down here. I'd do anything to come back home."

Shawn went to bed early. He felt exhausted from running in the rain and getting lost and from such a frightening afternoon. He kept picturing the wall of tiny skulls. And he kept hearing Ranger Saul's warning: "Be careful. Be *very* careful."

Shawn was just drifting off to sleep when he heard the howls outside his window.

He sat straight up, instantly alert. He could feel his muscles tensing, his whole body stiff with fright.

A long, mournful howl poured into the room from his open bedroom window. He held his breath and listened.

"Shawn . . . Shawn . . ."

Someone whispered his name. He hugged himself to keep from shivering. He sat up. Dropped his feet to the floor. Turned his gaze to the window. Only darkness out there. Like a black curtain. No moonlight at all.

Shawn . . . Shawn . . . Shawn . . ."

"Who . . . who is out there?" He tried to shout but the words came out in a whisper.

Is it Zeke? Is it Decker?

"Shawn . . . Shawn . . ."

He forced himself to stand. His legs were trembling, but he made them move. Across his small room. Out into the hall. To Kelli's room.

Kelli, I need your help.

He pushed open the door without knocking. He dove across the room to her bed. And let out a sharp cry.

She was GONE.

15

Shawn stood in a square of gray light, staring at Kelli's empty bed. The covers were tangled. The pillow was creased.

He gasped as he heard a sound behind him. A soft footstep.

I'm not alone in here.

He spun to the door — and let out a cry.

Kelli stood in the doorway, her nightshirt down to the floor, her hair wild about her face. "Shawn? What are you doing in my room?"

"I . . . I had to see you. I . . ." he stammered. "Where *were* you?"

"In the kitchen," she said. She raised a glass of water in one hand. "Getting a drink. It's so hot tonight." She saw the frantic expression on her brother's face, the wide eyes, the trembling chin. "Shawn, what's your problem?"

"It . . . it's out there," Shawn stuttered.

Kelli narrowed her eyes at him. "*What* is out there? You heard something?"

He nodded. "The Shaggedy. It's come for me, Kelli. It's out there and it's come for me."

"Were you dreaming?" she asked. "Having a nightmare?"

He shook his head. "It called my name. It kept calling me. It's out there. It knows my name and — and —" He trembled violently.

Kelli scrambled into her sneakers. "Stay here," she told Shawn, motioning with both hands. "Stay in the house. I'll see what's going on."

"No. Kelli —" He reached for her but she slipped out of his grasp. "Don't go out there. Please —"

But she was already to the door. She pushed it open and darted into the steamy, hot night. Greeted by a symphony of chirping crickets and tree frogs. The hot wind making her nightshirt swirl.

She ran to the side of the little house. She could see Shawn's open bedroom window in the back, the curtains fluttering inside the room.

"Who's there?" Kelli called, her voice hollow on the night air. "Who's there? Is anyone out here?"

In the shifting breeze, the tall swamp grass swayed one way, then the other. The trees at the back, tall on their stilted roots, shook and made whispering sounds.

Despite the heat, a chill ran down Kelli's back. She froze when she heard a cough. A crackle of dried weeds on the ground.

She saw something move behind the thicket of trees at the end of the yard. A flash of black moving quickly between the tilted tree trunks.

"Who's there?" Her voice cracked. She couldn't stop herself. She didn't think about the danger. She leaned into the wind and trotted toward the trees.

And saw him. Saw him clearly. Kneeling to the ground, examining a fallen tree limb.

"What are *you* doing out here?" The question burst from her throat.

Ranger Saul turned and looked up from the tree limb. His eyes were silvery in the dim light. He locked them on Kelli. "What are *you* doing out here?" He repeated her question. "It's not safe to be out in the swamp at night."

Again, his words didn't sound like friendly advice. They sounded to Kelli like a threat. And the way he stared at her without blinking, his expression so dark and grim, sent another chill down her back.

"I . . . know it isn't safe," she said, taking a step back, keeping her distance from this strange man. He was dressed all in black, as if he didn't want to be seen. A black hoodie covered his white hair.

They stared at each other in silence for a long moment. Saul climbed to his feet and brushed off the legs of his black pants with both hands.

"My brother heard noises," Kelli told him. "He says someone was whispering his name."

"Maybe he was dreaming," Saul said. "Is your brother scared down here? Is he scared all the time?"

"Pretty much," Kelli answered. "Were you whispering at Shawn's window?"

"Of course not," Saul replied. "Do you think I go around scaring people?"

"Then why are you out here behind my house in the middle of the night?" Kelli demanded. She brushed a large winged insect off her cheek.

A strange, unpleasant smile spread over Saul's bearded face. "Night is the best time to hunt in the swamp," he said.

"Hunt *what*?" Kelli asked.

His smile faded as fast as it had appeared. "That's *my* business," he snapped. He tightened the black hood around his head.

"Do you know about the Shaggedy?" Kelli blurted out. "You said you know everything about the swamp."

Saul's face lit up. "The Shaggedy? What have you heard?" he asked eagerly.

"Some kids at school say they saw it. I don't believe them."

Saul shook his head. "It's not a joke, Kelli. The Shaggedy is real."

"Huh? He's real? Have you seen him? What have you heard about him?"

Saul rubbed his beard. "The Shaggedy lives in a cavern in the deepest water. Down so far underwater, no one has ever been able to see anything but the purest blackness. He lives in his own world down there with many other strange swamp creatures."

Kelli studied Saul's face as he talked, trying to decide if he believed what he was telling her, or if he was making up a fairy tale to frighten her.

"Have you seen him?" she demanded. "These boys at school . . . They say they saw him when he came up from the water and walked around town."

"I've never seen him," Saul said. "I've read reports. And I've spoken to people who claim to have seen him."

A long, mournful bird cry made them both jump. Kelli heard the flapping of large wings in a tree above her head. The chirping of the crickets stopped for a moment, then picked up again, a steady, whistling drone in her ears.

"People have reported that the Shaggedy is half man, half monster," Saul continued. "He stands on two legs, taller than any man. His head is huge. His face is ugly, his features gross and deformed. He has hands and feet like a man, only larger. And his skin is reptilian, lined like lizard skin. Wherever he walks, he drips the muck and slime of the swamp."

Kelli realized her mouth was hanging open. She had been holding her breath as she listened to this frightening description. Now she let it out in a long whoosh.

She tried to picture the creature Saul had described. She imagined this half man, half reptile rising up from the swamp water and stomping onto land. And once again, she pictured the enormous footprints dug into the ground around her school.

"Do you want to know *all* about the Shaggedy?" Saul asked.

The crickets stopped chirping suddenly. The wind died. A hush fell over them. Kelli wanted to be inside her house. She didn't want to be out here in the woods with this frightening man, listening to this story about a living swamp monster.

She knew she should call her father. She knew she should go inside. But instead, she said, "Yes. Go on." She had to know everything.

"This is the legend," Saul began. "If you take the blood from a dead animal, and you use it to make fifty smears on a sheet of black paper . . . And if you yell ten times the words *Here comes the Shaggedy* . . . That's all it takes. Drip the blood fifty times and call his name, the Shaggedy will rise from the swamp. The creature will come to you and do whatever you tell it to."

Kelli thought about it for a moment. "The Shaggedy will be your slave?"

Saul nodded.

Kelli felt sweat run down her forehead. Sometimes the swamp was steamier at night than during the day.

"Do you believe that story?" she demanded.

Saul nodded. "I believe everything I hear about this swamp."

Kelli squinted at him. "And you really believe if someone takes fifty drops of blood —"

"Everything," Saul repeated. "I believe everything."

And before Kelli could react, he suddenly dove forward. Lurched toward the trees. Swiped his hand low — and grabbed a long, fat snake off the fallen tree limb.

The snake hissed in protest. Snapped its jaws. Once. Again.

The snake curled itself around Saul's arm. Saul grunted as he wrestled with it. It snapped its fangs at his wrist. Just missed.

Saul tightened his grip, then snapped the snake's head back. The snake uttered a faint hiss and went limp. Saul held it tightly in one hand, his grip just below the big snake's head.

Kelli struggled to catch her breath. The wrestling match had been terrifying. "How did you do that?" she cried. "How did you see that snake in the dark?"

Saul kept his eyes on the snake. "I've been in the swamp so long," he said, "I can see like a snake."

He's not normal, Kelli thought. *The way he moves. The way he prowls around. The way he likes to KILL. Saul is like a swamp monster himself.*

"Uh . . . I'd better get back inside," she stammered. "My brother was so scared. I have to tell him it was you out here — not a swamp monster."

Saul nodded. He wrapped the snake tighter around his arm. "Take care," he said. "No one is truly safe here." He turned and disappeared into the darkness behind the slender trees.

Kelli hurried back to the house. Her head was spinning with pictures — dark, frightening pictures. Again, she saw Saul grabbing a snake in the dark. And she pictured the Shaggedy, half man, half creature, rising up on the surface of the water.

Like a horror movie, she thought. *Swamp Beast III. But now we're living in it!*

The next morning was Thursday. Kelli woke up feeling really hungry. She stepped into the kitchen to make pancakes. Her dad sat at the small kitchen table, reading the news on his iPad. Coffee was bubbling in the coffeemaker. Shawn wandered in, still in his pajamas, yawning and stretching.

"You look like something the cat dragged in," his dad told him. "What's your problem, Shawn?"

"We don't have a cat," Shawn said.

Their dad frowned at him. "It's an expression. What do cats usually drag in? Dead mice, maybe. Dead birds . . ."

"It's a dumb expression," Shawn said.

"I can see you're in a great mood," his dad said.

"I couldn't get back to sleep," Shawn told Kelli. "I was too scared. I was up all night."

Dad set his iPad down on the table. "What happened? Why were you scared?"

"Shawn heard voices outside his window," Kelli answered. "Someone calling his name. I didn't want to wake you. You're such a sound sleeper, it's *impossible* to wake you anyway. So I went outside and looked around."

"And?" her dad asked.

"And . . . it was that creepy guy. Saul, the guy who said he was a park ranger."

Her dad squinted at her. "Really? He was outside our house?"

Kelli nodded. "Prowling around in the trees, looking for snakes, I think. He said he didn't whisper Shawn's name or anything."

"Do you think you had one of your nightmares, Shawn?" his Dad asked.

Shawn shrugged. "It didn't seem like a nightmare." He turned to Kelli. "I don't want pancakes. I just want cereal."

"Are you going to be difficult all day?" Kelli asked him.

He nodded. "Definitely." He pulled open the fridge door. "Hey, there's no milk."

"Would you two run and get some?" their dad asked. "Walk to that little general store on the path behind our house. It'll only take five minutes. You'll still have plenty of time to get to school."

"No problem," Kelli said. She lowered a stack of pancakes onto her dad's plate. He handed her a five-dollar bill. "Hurry back."

Kelli motioned to Shawn. "Quick. Get out of your pajamas and get dressed."

He groaned. "Why can't you go? Why do I have to go, too?"

"Because I'd miss you," Kelli teased.

A few minutes later, they stepped out the front door. The morning sun was still a red ball just above the trees. The swamp grass shimmered, still wet from the early dew.

The path to the little store was not far behind their yard. Kelli turned and led the way along the side of the house.

"Oh, wow." Shawn stopped and grabbed her arm. "Oh, wow."

They both froze and stared in shock at the ground in front of Shawn's bedroom window . . . stared at the two huge footprints sunk deep in the grass.

16

"I knew it," Shawn murmured. "I knew the Shaggedy was here. Those are the same footprints we saw around school."

Kelli stared wide-eyed at the round prints dug deep in the ground.

They heard someone approaching, and turned to see their dad trotting after them. "What's up?" he asked. He blinked as he saw the two footprints. "Whoa."

He squatted low and studied one of them, running his fingers along the smooth dirt. "Can't be real," he muttered. "No way."

"They're real," Shawn insisted in a trembling voice. "It came for me. Last night. I heard it whispering my name. The Shaggedy was here last night."

Their dad climbed to his feet. "No, Shawn —" he started.

But Shawn did his shoulder thing and went

very pale. "We . . . can't stay here, Dad," he stammered.

Dad put a hand on Shawn's shoulder. "It isn't real, Shawn. It has to be a joke. Do you want me to go talk to those two boys from your school? They must be the ones trying to frighten you."

"NO!" Shawn cried. "No, Dad. That would only make it harder for us. This isn't a joke. Look at these footprints. The Shaggedy was here last night. I know it was." His whole body shuddered.

"Maybe he's right," Kelli said softly. "Maybe it's too scary here. Maybe we should go back home."

Their dad hugged Shawn. He ignored Kelli's remark. "I have an idea," he said. "Something to take your minds off all this monster talk. It's a beautiful day. Let's take a boat ride on the river."

"A boat ride?" Shawn's eyes grew wide with fright.

Their dad waved a hand. "No fishing. Just a calm, smooth ride. Forget school today. Go back inside, get changed, and we'll take the boat out. I promise you'll enjoy it."

Shawn continued to eye him. "Promise?"

His dad raised his right hand. "I promise."

The clear blue sky reflected in the water as they let their boat drift with the river current. The sun warmed the morning air. Two red hawks swooped gracefully overhead.

Kelli smiled and tilted her head back, feeling the sun on her face. A large black-and-yellow butterfly fluttered over her face, then darted away.

"That's a swallowtail butterfly," her dad said. "Beautiful markings. They are tropical butterflies."

He turned to Shawn. "Are you feeling calmer? What are you staring at?"

Shawn leaned over the side, gazing down into the water. "An orange snake," he said. "It's way big. Look, Dad."

"It's a salt marsh water snake," his dad said, catching sight of it. "It won't bother you."

"I'm keeping my hands inside the boat," Shawn said.

His dad snickered. "You're getting smart."

They began to row as the current slowed. The water grew darker.

"Getting into deep water now," their dad told them. "We're lucky it's so calm today. We're very close to Deep Hole. The most exciting and mysterious part of the river."

A sudden wave rocked the little boat. Shawn cried out. Kelli gripped the sides.

The world's deepest cavern, she thought. *It's right beneath us now.*

Her mouth dropped open and she pointed with a trembling finger. "Dad — look. Something is bubbling in the water."

"Huh?" Shawn gasped.

Their dad lowered his oars. "I don't see anything, Kelli."

"Don't you see it? It's kind of churning, splashing back and forth. Like something is right below the surface."

"No!" Shawn screamed. "Let's get *away* from here!"

Their dad flashed Kelli a stern look. "Stop scaring your brother. I mean it." He gazed at the water. "I don't see what you are talking about. All rivers have currents, Kelli."

"It . . . didn't look like a current. Seriously," she replied. "The water was churning. Like something was coming up."

Their dad sighed. "That's enough. You two are determined to live in a horror movie. Did you forget you're New Yorkers? You're not supposed to be afraid of anything."

"Remind us when we get back to New York," Kelli said.

They rowed back home in silence.

Shawn kept his head down, his eyes on the water. Kelli hummed softly to herself. She saw a bunch of little dark brown rabbits hunched on a spit of sand that jutted into the water. "What are those, Dad?"

"They're called Lower Keys marsh rabbits."

"They're so cute," she said.

Her dad didn't answer. He seemed to be thinking hard about something. She wondered if he was thinking at all about going back to New York.

At home, Kelli disappeared into her room.

Shawn strode to the refrigerator. "What do we have for lunch, Dad?"

Before his father could answer, they both heard a shrill shout.

"Dad! Shawn! Help me!" Kelli screamed from her room. "Help me! It's the Shaggedy! The Shaggedy!"

17

Dr. Andersen and Shawn darted down the short hall to Kelli's room. She stood in the middle of the room, eyes wide with shock, both hands tugging at her hair.

"Whoa." Her dad uttered a low cry of surprise. The room had been trashed, completely torn apart. Her mattress was off the bed, tilted on its side. Big red footprints, still wet, crossed the carpet. Clothes were strewn everywhere.

"Dad, look!" Shawn cried, pointing to the back wall.

Scrawled in huge, red painted letters were the words:

I'M COMING FOR YOU BOTH!

Her hands still grasping her hair, Kelli turned to her father. "Dad, it's real! It's real! It's the Shaggedy. This isn't a joke!"

Kelli's dad moved to hug her. He glimpsed Shawn trembling in the doorway, his eyes locked

84

on the scrawled message smeared across the bedroom wall.

"Calm down, Kelli," he said softly. "Calm down. Take a deep breath." His expression turned to anger. "Those two boys from your school have gone too far this time."

Kelli took a step back from him. "But, Dad —"

"This is breaking and entering," their father said, gazing at the destruction. "This is a serious crime. I want you two to stay here. I'm going to deal with this."

He spun away and stomped into the hall, swinging both fists at his side.

"Dad, wait!" Kelli called. "What are you going to do?"

"Stay here," he ordered. He stepped outside and slammed the door behind him.

Shawn hesitated, but Kelli moved quickly. She opened the door and followed her dad outside. She watched him making his way to the trees at the back of the house. He was taking long, angry strides, his hands curled into fists.

She hung back, staying in the shadow of the house. She knew he was taking the path that led to the school. Her heart pounding, she followed. She stayed far behind him, trying to walk in the shadows of the tall, tilting trees.

He glanced back once. She ducked behind a low pine shrub. He didn't see her. She followed him all the way to school.

When he went inside, Kelli crept up to the classroom window. She could see her dad talking and motioning to Miss Rawls. He pointed to Zeke and Decker.

Kelli realized she was holding her breath. She let it out in a long whoosh.

A few seconds later, the school door opened and her dad appeared, followed by the twins. Kelli pressed herself against the wall of the building, close enough to hear everything.

"Why aren't Kelli and Shawn in school today?" Zeke asked.

"Never mind that," her dad said. "I think you know why I need to speak to you."

The boys glanced at one another again, then turned back to Dr. Andersen, their faces blank.

"A joke is a joke," Kelli's dad said, keeping his voice steady and calm. "But this time you've gone too far."

"Excuse me?" Zeke squinted at him, his freckled nose twitching.

"Huh?" Decker echoed.

"I think you know —" Dr. Andersen started. But a frantic shout made him stop.

"Dad! Don't! Dad — please stop!"

Kelli came running up to them, breathing hard, her face red, hair tangled around her head.

"Dad — stop!" she cried again, grabbing his wrist.

"Kelli, what is your problem?" he said. "I have to put an end to this once and for all. These two boys —"

"No," Kelli said, struggling to catch her breath. "You don't understand. Zeke and Decker didn't do it, Dad. *I* did it!"

18

Kelli had to choke out the words. It felt as if her heart had leaped into her throat. She struggled to breathe as she confessed again. "I did it all, Dad. Zeke and Decker don't know what you're talking about."

Her dad's mouth hung open. Behind his glasses, his eyes were wide, locked on Kelli.

Miss Rawls poked her head out the door. "Everything okay?"

"These boys can go back inside," Dr. Andersen told her, his eyes still on Kelli. "I'm so sorry for the interruption."

Zeke and Decker hurried back into the school, grins on their faces. Zeke turned at the doorway and made a face at Kelli, flashing her a thumbs-down.

Kelli sighed and looked away.

"Please explain," her father said softly.

Kelli shrugged. "I did everything. I wrote that message on my backpack. I put the water and the note in Shawn's locker. Last night after you went to bed, I took your shovel and I dug the two footprints under Shawn's window. Then I stood outside, whispering his name. Then . . . then . . ." Her voice cracked.

"Then you trashed your own room?" her dad demanded.

She nodded. She fought back the tears that began to form in her eyes. She was determined not to cry. "Yes. Before we went on the boat ride. I trashed my own room and wrote the thing about the Shaggedy on my wall."

She kept her eyes down. She didn't want to see her dad's expression.

She waited for him to explode. But he remained quiet. "Why?" he asked in a whisper. "Kelli, why?"

She was the one to explode. "Because I hate it here so much. Because I miss Marci and my other friends. Because they're all totally forgetting about me. They don't even text me. It's like I've disappeared."

"I . . . I don't understand," her dad said. "You wanted to scare Shawn?"

"I . . . I thought . . ." Kelli cleared her throat. "I thought if I could scare Shawn really badly . . . If I could make Shawn think the Shaggedy was real and that the Shaggedy was coming to get him . . . If I could really scare him . . . I thought you would see how terrified Shawn was, and you would take us all back to New York."

She slowly raised her eyes to her dad. His stare was angry and intense. But he didn't say a word. He mopped sweat off his bald head with one hand. And kept his gaze unblinking on her.

"I guess it was a really stupid plan," Kelli murmured.

He nodded. "Yes. Very stupid. And very harmful to your brother."

"And harmful to my room," Kelli joked, trying to get him to end his intense stare. "It will take me *hours* to get it back together."

"Well, you'll have plenty of time for that," her father said. "You're grounded forever."

Kelli shrugged. "What difference does it make? I don't have any friends here, and there's nothing to do anyway."

Her dad pointed to the path. "Just go home and clean up your room. I don't want any more attitude from you. And be sure to apologize to your brother."

Kelli turned and slumped away, her head down, her mind racing with angry thoughts. Yes, she had messed up. She knew she had messed up badly.

Oh, well, at least that's the end of the Shaggedy, Kelli thought. *That's the end of scaring poor Shawn.*

She was wrong about both.

19

"Let's stop right here by these mangrove trees," Miss Rawls said.

Kelli walked near the front of the line of kids, beside Shawn. *Those trees are totally creepy*, she thought. Their roots stuck up from the ground and spread over the dirt. Slender tendril-like branches hung from their lower limbs like legs.

"Those trees look like they could walk away," Kelli murmured.

"Stop making everything scary," Shawn scolded. "Haven't you tried to scare me enough?"

Shawn was right. She had acted terribly. And selfishly. He had good reason to be angry with her.

She knew it was her job to make it up to Shawn, to make sure he got over his fear of the swamp.

Once a week, Miss Rawls and Mrs. Klavan, the other teacher, walked everyone in the school to the river. The idea was to explore and to learn to identify the plants and animals in the swamp.

Even though it was morning, the air felt steamy and hot. The heat seemed to radiate from the marshy ground. *As if we were walking on top of hot coals*, Kelli thought.

Miss Rawls raised a bunch of papers in one hand. "Does everyone have a worksheet?" she called. She waited for everyone to pull them out of their backpacks. "Make a check mark in front of the plants you identify. And people, don't wander too far. Stay in groups, okay? Mrs. Klavan and I don't want to be searching the trees all day."

Kelli and Shawn studied their worksheets. "Four-petal pawpaws," Kelli murmured. "They shouldn't be too hard to find." She read the names of the other two plants out loud: "Golden aster and swamp lily."

Kids split into groups and began walking in different directions, following the paths through the tall, swaying reeds and low pine shrubs.

"Let's follow the path away from those weird trees," Shawn said, pointing.

Kelli gazed at the sandy path. It curled around the shore of the river, back into a thicket of slender flowering trees. The river water sparkled under the morning sun. The slow current made a trickling sound as it rolled past them.

Shawn swatted a big fly off the back of his hand. "Ow. It *bit* me."

"I'm sure you were delicious," Kelli said.

"Look. I have a red bump."

She grinned at him. "Want me to kiss it and make it better?"

"Shut up, stupid."

They followed the path. It led away from the water, through a wall of tall reeds. Kelli heard a scraping sound. Soft thuds. The footsteps of small animals darting along the bottoms of the reeds. Swamp mice?

She and Shawn stopped when they heard a louder sound. The crackle of dry leaves. Heavy thuds on the ground. They froze and listened.

And cried out when the tall reeds parted. And Zeke and Decker pushed their way onto the path in front of them. Their white-blond hair glowed in the bright sunlight. Their faces were red, angry.

"You're not supposed to leave the group," Zeke said.

Kelli glanced around. "We didn't realize we'd wandered off so far," she said.

Despite the heat, the twins wore dark blue hoodies, hoods pushed back, over their denim cargo shorts. They moved to block the path.

"What's up with your dad?" Decker demanded. "What is his problem, anyway?" He spit the words angrily.

"Well . . ." Kelli didn't know what to say.

"Why did he accuse Decker and me like that?" Zeke asked. "Why did he pull us out of school and say we did things to scare you?"

Kelli swallowed. Her mouth suddenly felt dry. "It was all a big mix-up," she said. "Sorry —"

"Mix-up?" Decker said, squinting at her. "What's a mix-up? When someone's father drags you out of school for something you didn't do? That's a mix-up?" He tensed his fists at his sides.

Kelli felt a shiver run down her back. *I didn't think these guys would be so angry.*

"I . . . I'm sorry," she said. "Really. Please accept my apology."

They exchanged glances. Zeke's scowl faded. "Okay," he said finally. "Apology accepted."

Shawn interrupted. "So does that mean you won't try to scare us about the Shaggedy anymore?"

Zeke stuck his face up close to Shawn's. He ignored Shawn's question. "Want to see the coolest place in the swamp?" he asked.

"N-not really," Shawn stammered, shoving his hands into his shorts pockets.

"Come on," Decker said, giving Shawn a gentle push. "Follow us. It's not dangerous. It's way cool."

"Way cool," Zeke echoed. "Come on. You'll like it. Hurry. Before Miss Rawls sees us. This place is amazing. Trust us." He smiled. "Now that we're friends, we'll show it to you."

Decker nodded. "Yeah. Now that we're friends . . ."

20

The path curled away from the river. But Zeke and Decker led Kelli and her brother off the path, into the underbrush of vine tendrils and fat vine leaves.

"Where are you taking us? This is pretty far," Kelli said.

Decker bumped her from behind. "You'll see. You won't believe it. It's wild."

"Miss Rawls will be looking for us," Shawn said. He tripped over a thick vine tendril. Decker caught him and kept him from falling.

They squeezed through a thicket of tightly tangled trees — and found themselves gazing at a part of the river they hadn't seen before. A spit of sand stretched out into the water, curving to form a perfect circle.

"That's it," Zeke said, suddenly excited. "See? The sand forms a circle. And inside the circle is Monster Hole."

"Huh? Monster Hole?" Shawn's voice cracked. Kelli put her hands on his shoulders.

"That's where we saw it," Decker said. "That's where we saw the Shaggedy for the *second* time."

Kelli squinted at him. "The *second* time?"

Both boys nodded. "The first time was when he pounded on our neighbor's door," Zeke said. "After that night, Decker and I kept watch. And we saw it again." He pointed. "We watched it rise up from the water right there."

Shawn made a gulping sound. "You're joking, right? You're not serious?"

Zeke raised his right hand. "I swear."

"He just popped up in the water," Decker said, "with all this gunk pouring off him. Like mud and leaves and stuff. He wiped it out of his hair, and he started to move toward the shore. To right where we're standing."

Kelli studied the two boys. They didn't appear to be joking. Were they making the story up as they went along? They were so serious. So intense.

Could they be telling the truth?

"The Shaggedy climbed out of the swamp," Zeke said. "He was huge. I mean, like the Incredible Hulk from the comic books. Only he was covered in lizard skin."

"He stomped onto the sand," Decker continued the story. "Zeke and I hid behind those trees over there. And we watched the Shaggedy climb

96

onto the shore. He had huge webbed feet. He walked over to that tree, and he grabbed a squirrel off a tree limb. Just reached out and grabbed it in his huge hand."

Shawn made the gulping sound again. Kelli saw that he was trembling in fright. She knew she should shut the boys up. But she wanted to hear the end of the story.

"He ate the squirrel in one bite," Zeke said. "I'll never forget the sound the squirrel made when the Shaggedy bit into it. It *squeaked*. Did you ever hear a squirrel squeak?"

"It ate the squirrel," Decker said, "and squirrel juice ran down the monster's chin. It licked its big lips. Then it turned and thudded back into the water on its webbed feet. It just kept walking until it sank under the surface, and it didn't come back up."

"That's where it came up," Zeke said, pointing into the circle of river water again. "That's where we saw it. Decker and I ... we've been kind of obsessed ever since. You see why?"

"No," Kelli said. "I don't see why. I think it's just a story that everyone in this town repeats."

Actually, Kelli didn't know *what* to believe. Ranger Saul had told her about the Shaggedy. And these two boys talked about nothing else. But the monster couldn't be real. It couldn't.

She kept her hands on Shawn's shoulders. "Look how he's shaking. What's the big thrill from scaring him with a dumb monster story?" she demanded.

Zeke's blue eyes flashed. "You think it's a dumb story? Seriously?"

Kelli nodded. "Yes, I do."

"You think it's all made it up?" Decker said.

"Yes, I do," Kelli repeated.

"Well, why don't you go check it out for yourselves?" Zeke cried.

He and his brother lowered their heads and charged at Kelli and Shawn. Butted them hard — and sent them flying into the water.

The river was deep here. Kelli and Shawn splashed down hard. They both sank below the surface, then came up thrashing and gasping for air.

"That's for sending your father to accuse us!" Zeke declared.

Kelli and Shawn struggled toward shore. But the river current pushed them back.

"Oh, wow. Here it comes!" Decker shouted, gazing past them. "The Shaggedy! It's right behind you!"

21

Kelli froze for a moment. She started to sink. Taking a deep breath, she spun around in the water.

Nothing there.

Zeke and his twin had tossed back their heads, laughing hard, slapping high fives.

Shawn had his face in the water. He was stroking hard, struggling to reach shore. Kelli wrapped her arm around his waist to help him move forward.

She climbed out first, then turned to pull him onto the sand.

"What's going on here?" Miss Rawls came running from the trees. Her eyes were wide with shock. "Did you fall in?"

"These new kids were goofing around," Zeke answered quickly. "They were wrestling each other and they fell in."

"Zeke and I were helping to pull them out," Decker chimed in.

Liars, thought Kelli. She tugged a limp vine tendril from her hair. Then she squeezed water from her T-shirt, knotting it in front of her.

A group of kids had gathered to watch.

"Kelli and Shawn, you were very careless," Miss Rawls said. "I'm very disappointed in you both."

Kelli saw the wide grins on the faces of Zeke and Decker.

"Oh no!" Shawn cried suddenly. He was staring at Kelli's legs. "What *are* those things?"

Kelli's legs itched like crazy. She glanced down. She saw several fat black worms stuck up and down both legs.

"Leeches," Miss Rawls said. "You've picked up some leeches, Kelli. They suck your blood."

Kelli couldn't help it. She opened her mouth in a scream. "I can *feel* it!" she cried. "I can feel them drinking my blood. Ouch. Oh, ouch. It hurts!"

Miss Rawls motioned with both hands. "Come over here. Mrs. Klavan and I will pull them off."

Kelli limped over to the two teachers. They squatted down and began removing leeches from Kelli's legs. Each leech made a sick *popping* sound as its sucker was loosened from her skin.

The rest of the students stood and watched. Some were laughing and making jokes. Some watched in silence, totally horrified by what they were seeing.

"Leech Girl! Hey — Leech Girl!" a boy shouted.

Some kids laughed.

Kelli was forcing herself not to cry. Her legs prickled and itched. She saw blood trickling down her calves.

Zeke and Decker had big grins frozen on their faces. *A total win for them today*, Kelli thought bitterly. *A total win.*

Kelli felt so sorry for herself. Things couldn't get any worse — *could* they?

22

The next morning, Kelli tried to text her friend Marci in New York. But Marci didn't answer.

"She probably has a whole bunch of new friends," Kelli told herself sadly. "She's forgetting all about me."

Even though it was early, the morning air was steamy and hot. *I'm sick of this hot, humid weather*, she thought. *I'm sick of waking up every morning already sweaty.* She sighed. *I'm sick of everything down here.*

She pulled on a sleeveless T-shirt and a pair of white shorts. She didn't bother to brush her hair. *No one cares what I look like.*

Kelli started to the kitchen for breakfast. But Shawn stopped her in the hall. He raised his phone to her. "You'd better take a look at this," he said softly.

She took the phone and gazed at the screen. "What is this, Shawn? Someone's Instagram?"

Her heart stopped beating as the photo on the

screen came into focus. There she was, standing on the edge of the swamp, her mouth open in a scream. She could see the disgusting black leeches up and down her legs.

She read the caption in a trembling voice:

"Leech Girl Rises from Monster Hole."

Kelli forced herself to look away from the screen. She had never felt so angry in her life. Angry and sad and embarrassed at the same time. She could feel the blood pulsing at her temples. She really thought her head might explode.

She handed the phone back to Shawn without saying a word.

But the angry thoughts flew through her brain. She pictured Zeke and Decker's grinning faces. *Now I'm going to be known as Leech Girl for the rest of the year.*

She stayed in the hall, hands balled into fists, struggling to calm down. But there was no way she could calm down. She was a total loser down here. She was a joke at school. She hadn't made a single new friend. Zeke and his twin made her life miserable. And all the frightening talk about the Shaggedy . . .

Suddenly, standing in the hall, her jaw clenched, her heart pounding, fists curled tightly, she knew what she had to do. She couldn't go on this way. She had to change things. And she knew how.

* * *

Kelli didn't tell Shawn her plan till after school. A pair of fat bog frogs scampered across the path as they made their way toward home. "Bet I could catch them," Shawn said. "Keep them as pets."

Kelli didn't reply. She was thinking about other things. Kids had called her Leech Girl all day. She heard them snickering and whispering every time she walked by.

She wanted to go roaring into them and wrestle them to the floor. But that was stupid. She had a better revenge plan than that.

"I'm going to call up the Shaggedy," she told Shawn.

His mouth dropped open. "Excuse me?"

"You heard me. I'm going to call up the Shaggedy."

He squinted at her. "You mean you *believe* in it?"

Kelli shrugged. "I don't know. Maybe I do. I'm going to follow that weird Ranger Saul's instructions. And I'm going to summon it up from the swamp."

"And then what?" Shawn demanded.

"Saul said if I called it up, it would do whatever I wanted."

"And what do you want it to do, Kelli?"

She shrugged again. "I don't really know. Scare Zeke and Decker out of their minds? Chase them out of town, maybe?"

Shawn laughed. "I don't believe you. You're joking, right?"

"No. I'm totally serious," Kelli said.

Shawn studied her. "And you want to call up a terrifying swamp monster from the under the water because . . . ?"

"Because I want to change things," Kelli said. "Because I don't want to be Leech Girl for the rest of the year. Because . . ."

Something in front of them on the path caught her eye. "Shawn, look." She pointed. A dead bird on its side on the dirt path. A large black bird with red markings on its wings and tail. Its tiny black eye gazed blankly up at the sky.

"We need fifty drops of blood," Kelli murmured. She bent to pick up the dead bird. "Maybe it has the blood we need. Come on, Shawn. Let's do this!"

23

Kelli cradled the dead bird in both hands and carried it to their house. The bird was still warm. She really hoped it had the fifty drops of blood inside it that she needed.

"This is crazy," Shawn insisted. "Please don't do this, Kelli."

"It's bigger than crazy!" she exclaimed. "It's stupendous! It's incredible!" A wave of excitement made her whole body tingle.

She put a hand on his shoulder. "I know you're scared. But just think, Shawn . . . If this doesn't work and it turns out there's no such thing as a Shaggedy, you won't have to worry about it anymore."

She thought that might calm him down. Or at least shut him up. But it didn't work at all.

"Please don't do this," he said again, tugging her arm. "Please."

"Okay, okay. You made your point," she told him. "I know what your opinion is. But I'm going to do it anyway. You can either come along and help me. Or you can stay home and hide under the bed or something. And you'll miss all the incredible excitement."

He stared at her, his face tense, his fists in his pockets. Finally, he let out a long sigh. "Okay. I'll go with you." His voice broke. "It won't work, anyway, right? Right?"

"Well . . . there's only one way to find out," Kelli murmured. She handed him a sheet of black paper. Then she pulled a sharp steak knife from the silverware drawer.

"Wh-what are you going to do with that knife?" Shawn stammered.

Kelli frowned at him. "We have to get the blood out of the bird, don't we?"

She handed him the sheet of black paper. Then she cradled the dead bird in one arm. She carried the knife in her free hand.

They stepped out of their house, walked back along the side, and took the path that led to the swamp. The late afternoon sun kept ducking behind clouds. Long shadows formed in front of them, then vanished when the sunlight faded.

There was no wind. The trees and shrubs were still. A lone bird crying high above them was the only sound Kelli heard, except for the soft *thud* of their sandals on the dirt path.

They turned at the river and followed the path that led around to Monster Hole. No one around. Total silence now. Even the crickets were silent.

The river water was dark gray with dull patches of green under the cloudy sky. The current was gentle, lapping softly on the muddy shore.

Kelli squinted at the sandbar that circled Monster Hole. The sun appeared again and made the water sparkle. Shawn held the black paper stiffly in front of him. "Are we really doing this?"

"Don't talk," Kelli said. "Just try to be helpful."

She took the paper from him and set it down flat on the dirt. "Hold it down. Don't let it blow away."

"There's no wind," Shawn said.

"Don't argue, Shawn. Just hold the paper down." Kelli didn't mean to sound so sharp with her brother. She realized she was tense. Her whole body felt tight, as if all her muscles had been tied in knots.

She dropped to her knees and placed the bird on its back on the ground. The slender legs stood stiffly straight up. The blank-eyed head tilted at a strange angle. The feathers felt stiff and dry.

Kelli raised the knife over the bird. "I hope it still has its blood," she murmured.

"I can't look." Shawn covered his eyes with one hand.

Kelli didn't reply. She tightened her grip on the steak knife handle, lowered the blade to the bird. Then she brought her hand down fast, dug the blade in deep, and made a long cut down the middle of the bird's belly.

She had this weird feeling that the bird would utter a shrill scream. But, of course, it remained silent and didn't move. And as she gazed down at the deep cut she had made, a trickle of dark blood oozed onto the smooth, feathery belly.

"Yes!" she cried, pumping a fist in the air.

"Sick," Shawn muttered. He held the paper down with both hands.

Kelli set the knife down next to the bird. Then she dipped her pointer finger into the trickling blood. "Fifty drops onto the paper," she told Shawn. "Then we call out the Shaggedy's name ten times. And we'll see what happens."

"Uh . . . yeah. We'll see," Shawn murmured. His eyes were on the gently rolling water. He didn't want to look at the cut-open dead bird.

Drip drip drip drip.

Kelli counted silently to herself. The blood felt warm on her finger. When it stopped trickling over the side of the cut, she had to dig her finger into the bird's body to get more.

"Hurry up," Shawn urged. "This is making me sick. Seriously."

"Everything makes you sick," Kelli murmured.

Drip drip drip . . .

The bird's belly had fallen open. It looked as if the poor bird had cracked in half. Kelli dripped

109

the last few drops of blood onto the paper. "Okay." She jumped to her feet. "Bring the paper closer to the water, Shawn."

He held back. "No. *You* do it. It's totally yucky."

She rolled her eyes and took the paper from his hand. "Follow me." She led the way to the water's edge. The ground grew soft and muddy here. Water lapped in a soft, steady rhythm.

Shawn stayed a few steps behind Kelli. "Can you at least help me shout his name?" she asked.

He nodded. "Okay."

They began to shout in unison. "Here comes the Shaggedy! Here comes the Shaggedy! Here comes the Shaggedy!"

Their voices rang over the deep water. Kelli cupped her hands around her mouth and shouted even louder. "Here comes the Shaggedy! Here comes the Shaggedy! Here comes the Shaggedy! Here comes the Shaggedy! Here comes the Shaggedy! Here comes the Shaggedy! Here comes the Shaggedy!"

Ten times.

Kelli gazed around the circle of water that formed Monster Hole. The sun slid behind clouds again. The river water faded to gray.

"Nothing happening," Shawn said, standing three steps behind her. "This was stupid. Let's go home."

"Wait." Kelli motioned with one hand. "Just wait. And watch."

Kelli held her breath and stared at the dark, rolling river. Rolling smoothly. Nothing changing. Nothing interrupting the soft, steady flow of water.

Nothing happening . . .

She uttered a sigh. Maybe her brother was right. Maybe this was a dumb waste of time.

Clouds washed overhead. They made a shadow appear in the water.

No. Wait. The shadow wasn't caused by the clouds.

Kelli gasped and took a step to the water's edge. She stared wide-eyed straight ahead . . . into the middle of the circle . . . into the middle of Monster Hole.

And she saw the water start to swirl. Low waves rose against the current. Moving in the wrong direction. She heard a churning sound. The sound grew louder.

The water tossed up. Low waves smacked against waves. The water tossed and churned. The middle of the circle began to bubble.

Sunlight spread once again over the water, and Kelli could see clearly. See something below the surface . . . something rising in the water . . . rising rapidly as the water churned and bubbled.

She heard Shawn's frightened cry. He stepped up beside her and took her hand.

And they both watched the blue-green water appear to split apart . . . as the creature floated up . . . floated up over the surface. First its head, then its broad shoulders. The river tossed and crashed like thunder.

They both cried out as the monster blinked several times, water rolling off its face — and locked its dark-eyed gaze on Kelli and Shawn.

24

Its face was blue and puffy. Its eyes were an eerie yellow. Water rolled off its head, its bare shoulders. The creature appeared to grow taller as it rose in the water and began to stomp toward the shore.

It pulled a tangle of weeds from its long sea-green hair, hair down past its shoulders. Its mouth hung open in a silent roar. A slender, silvery fish slid out of one of its nostrils and splashed into the water.

"Run! Kelli! Run!" Shawn screamed. He spun away from the terrifying creature, his shoes pounding the soft ground.

Kelli turned to run. But then she stopped. She remembered Ranger Saul's words. The Shaggedy would rise out of the water and do whatever she asked it to do.

She was the boss. She was its master.

She took a deep breath and summoned all her

courage. She could still hear Shawn's footsteps as he ran away. But she was determined to stay.

I called it up. Now I will control it.

She crossed her arms tightly in front of her to stop her body from shivering. She clenched her jaw and watched the enormous man-creature stomp toward the shore.

Its bare chest was covered in thick brown fur. Its arms were powerful and long. Its massive hands hung below his knees. Its legs were the size of tree stumps, covered entirely in brown fur so thick, it looked like dark leggings.

It uttered a low grunt. Black river water spewed from its open mouth. It tilted back its huge head and spewed more water from deep in its gut. It came storming toward Kelli, moving slowly, heavily. It slapped the surface of the water with both open hands as it walked, sending up high waves on both sides.

Kelli's knees started to fold. Her whole body shuddered. But she returned the creature's stare and stood her ground.

"Follow me, Shaggedy!" She tried to scream, but her voice came out in a choked whisper.

The creature shook water off itself like a dog after a bath. It lowered its huge head, scraggly wet hair falling over its yellow eyes.

"I called for you, Shaggedy!" Kelli found her voice and screamed. "And now you must do what I tell you!"

The monster tilted its head to the sky and roared. The ugly sound drove birds from the trees. It shoved its hair off its eyes with both fur-covered hands and glared, unblinking, at Kelli.

It stomped onto the wet mud of the shore. Took a step toward her. Another pounding step.

"Stop!" Kelli cried. A wave of panic rolled down her body. "Shaggedy — stop!"

But it kept coming, its eyes on hers like two wet flashlight beams. Another silver fish poked out of one nostril. The monster curled and uncurled giant fists at its sides.

"Shaggedy — stop!" Kelli screamed.

Before she could move out of its way, the creature raised a big fist and shoved her. A hard shove in the side that sent her toppling to the ground.

Kelli landed hard. Pain shot up and down her body.

She turned and saw the creature stomping to the trees.

"Stop!" she cried, trying to force away the pain. "Stop right there! Where are you going? *Stop!*"

25

Kelli climbed to her feet. She could see the big creature striding through the trees. It followed the path toward town, ripping vines and shrubs out of the ground with both hands as it walked.

"Wait! Stop!" Kelli ran after it. "You are supposed to listen to me! Stop!"

The monster turned, an ugly scowl on its dark blue face, and grunted in reply.

Kelli ducked behind a tree. Was it going to turn back and come for her?

No. It clomped away, its huge feet digging deep holes in the soft ground.

Kelli held her breath. The creature smelled like rotten fish. She wondered if she'd ever get the smell from her nose. Or the sight of its frightening wet yellow eyes beaming at her.

Kelli stopped shouting at it. She could see that it wouldn't listen to her. She followed on trembling legs, keeping a safe distance. She wanted to scream for help, but there was no one in sight.

She wondered if Shawn had run all the way home. She wondered if he was telling her dad about the monster. Maybe her dad would come and . . .

The path led to a row of small white houses. Kelli stopped with a gasp as the creature strode up to the first house. It pulled its powerful arm back — and shoved a fist through the front window. Glass shattered. Someone inside the house screamed in shock.

The creature lifted a metal trash can off the ground and heaved it through the broken window.

"Stop! Oh, please — !" Kelli begged.

But the creature was already at the next house. It reached both hands up — and tore the gutter off the roof. It clanged to the ground. The creature lowered its shoulder to the front door and splintered it easily. The door cracked in half and tipped off of its hinges.

Kelli saw faces in the windows across the street. People heard the crashes and the shattering glass. She stood helplessly, watching the creature she had summoned go berserk. She had called it up, and now it was destroying everything in its path . . . wrecking everything — and enjoying it.

What have I done? Why did I do this?

The monster tugged a mailbox out of the ground and heaved it through the windshield of a dark blue pickup truck parked at the curb. Glass shattered and flew everywhere.

"Help!" Kelli shouted to the people watching from their houses. "Get help. Somebody — call the police!"

She heard a siren in the distance. Was help on the way?

Yes. A black-and-white patrol car came roaring up, red light flashing on its roof, siren blaring. It squealed to a stop. The front doors flew open, and two black-uniformed officers came leaping out.

The monster shoved over a slender tree. The tree cracked and crashed to the ground. Grunting hard, the monster turned its eyes on the approaching policemen.

They drew pistols. "Freeze!" one of them barked. "Don't move. Stay right there."

The creature dove for the officer, grabbed him around the waist, and tossed him aside. Before the other officer could react, the monster ducked its shoulders. It lifted the patrol car in both hands and heaved it into the house at the top of the yard.

Screams rang out. A crowd had gathered at the edge of the street. Dogs barked. The two officers stood frozen, watching the creature stomp through town, searching for more damage it could do.

Kelli turned — and saw Ranger Saul half-hidden behind a fat tree. He leaned into the tree trunk, watching. Not moving. Just watching.

Kelli took a deep breath and ran across the yards to Saul. "Help me!" she cried. "I . . . I called it up. I followed your instructions. I did everything you said."

She couldn't help her voice from trembling. Her whole body began to shake. "I did everything right," she choked out. "But the Shaggedy won't listen to me. The Shaggedy is going berserk. It's so horrible. He won't obey me at all."

Saul frowned and squinted hard at Kelli. "Shaggedy?" he said. "That's not the Shaggedy."

Kelli gasped. "I . . . don't understand."

"He doesn't look anything like the Shaggedy," Saul replied. "The Shaggedy is green with skin like a lizard. And the Shaggedy —"

He stopped and suddenly grabbed Kelli by the shoulders. He tugged her behind the tree.

Kelli felt the ground rumble as the monster stomped past them. She poked her head out from behind the tree and watched as the grunting creature returned to the path.

Keeping a safe distance, people trailed after him. Kelli and Saul followed. The monster never turned back. It took long, heavy strides, its big feet squashing plants and vines. It strode to the water and kept walking.

Kelli huddled close to Saul and watched as the creature appeared to sink under the slowly rolling river waters. Its chest . . . then its shoulders . . . then its head. The water churned as it vanished under the water.

The crowd of people all started talking at once. The two police officers stood on the shore, guns drawn, shaking their heads.

"He tossed my car a hundred feet," a man said.

"Who is going to pay for my house? He broke every window."

"I won't sleep a wink tonight. I'll be listening for that monster to come back."

"None of us are safe."

Kelli turned to Saul. "I followed the instructions. What did I do wrong?"

She spotted the sheet of black paper caught under a vine tendril. She picked it up and shoved it into his face. "What did I do wrong? Why isn't it the Shaggedy?"

Saul took the paper and squinted hard at it. He began to move his lips. Kelli figured out that he was counting the drips of bird blood.

Finally, Saul raised his eyes to her. "Only forty-eight droplets," he said. "You counted wrong."

"Oh, no." Kelli slapped her forehead. "I did it again. I . . . I hate *anything* to do with numbers."

Saul handed the sheet of paper back to her. "The legends say there are *dozens* of monsters who live deep in the bottom of Monster Hole. You called up a different monster, Kelli. You called up a monster you can't control."

Saul shook his head sadly. "He'll be back

121

tomorrow, and he'll destroy the whole town and everything in it."

Kelli's throat tightened. She forced herself to breathe. She fought back tears. "But . . . Saul . . . Isn't there anything we can do?"

He shook his head again. "No. I am afraid there isn't."

27

Saul snapped his fingers. "Except for maybe one thing. There might be something you can do."

Kelli grabbed his arm. "What? What is it?"

He frowned. "No. Forget it. It's too risky. Too dangerous."

"Saul, tell me," Kelli pleaded. "What happened today . . . It's all my fault. I want to do something to help. I'll do *anything*."

Saul glanced around. The shore was deserted now. Everyone had gone back to town. The sun was sinking behind the trees. The air suddenly grew cool.

"You're the only one who can try this," he told Kelli. "You called it up. The person who calls it up is the only person who can defeat this monster."

Kelli swallowed, her throat dry as cotton. "What do I have to do?"

Saul motioned to a rowboat tucked between two trees. "I'll row you out in that boat," he said. "To the middle of Monster Hole. The monster

123

will come up to the surface. He'll want to see who is there."

Saul reached into the leather pouch that hung from his belt. He pulled out a small cloth bag. "This is snake powder," he said. "I never go anywhere without it."

Kelli gazed at the bag in his hand. "What does it do?"

"You have to sprinkle this on the monster's head," he told her. "If you sprinkle it on his head, he will sink into the water. And he will never come on land again."

Kelli's brain spun. "You really think that will work?"

Saul nodded. "I think it will."

"Then come on," Kelli said, tugging his arm. "Let's go. Let's do it."

Her heart was racing so fast, she could barely breathe. But she forced her trembling legs to carry her to the rowboat.

As she started to climb in, she heard a shout. She spun around and saw Shawn running toward her from the path. "Shawn? Are you okay?" she cried. "Where's Dad?"

"Dad . . . is in town," he called breathlessly. He stopped beside the rowboat and lowered his hands to his knees, struggling to catch his breath. "I . . . I ran all the way. Dad is in town helping people whose houses were wrecked. He says for you to come home right away."

"I can't," Kelli said. "I have to go out in this boat with Ranger Saul. I have to do something about the monster." Her voice broke. "It . . . it's all my fault, Shawn."

Shawn stared at her. "What are you going to do?"

"I'll tell you when I get back," she said. She started to climb into the boat.

"No." Shawn grabbed her arm. "I'm going with you."

Kelli almost laughed. "Are you joking? You're terrified of water and terrified of being in a boat on the swamp."

"I . . . I know," Shawn answered. "But I won't let you go without me. We all have to be brave now."

Kelli nodded in agreement. "Okay. Jump in. But stay close to Saul. And hold on tight, okay?"

Shawn climbed in behind her. His eyes were wide with fright. But his jaw was set, and he didn't do his shoulder thing. Kelli could see that he was determined to be brave.

The sky darkened to charcoal. As Saul began to row, the river water was a deep purple. The current made rippling sounds as it rolled against the boat. Kelli felt as if the current was trying to push them back, telling them not to float out into Monster Hole.

She gripped the cloth bag of snake powder in one hand. Her eyes were on the tossing, dark water. No one spoke. In the distance, a bird cried, a high wail.

The boat rocked as they reached the deep water. Shawn gripped the sides so tightly, his hands were a pale white, even in the dying sunlight.

Kelli felt a wave of nausea roll down her stomach. Her throat tightened again. *Hope I don't barf.*

The cool night air made the skin on her arms tingle. She moved the cloth bag from hand to hand.

"We're just about in the middle of Monster Hole," Saul said in a low voice just above a whisper. He stopped rowing. The boat slid back and forth on the rolling current.

Kelli felt sick again. She swallowed rapidly. Held her breath. Peered down into the darkness of the deep water.

Will Saul's crazy scheme work?

She didn't have to wait long. The water began to churn violently. The rowboat rocked back. And Kelli could see a large, dark form floating up to the surface. As it came closer, she could see it clearly.

The monster . . . rising under the boat . . . about to crash into it from underneath . . . about to smash their boat and send them tumbling into the water.

126

28

Kelli opened her mouth to scream as the boat tossed back. Only a hoarse squeak escaped her throat. She rocked forward hard. So did Saul and Shawn. Then they were snapped back. The boat settled as the monster loomed up beside it.

Its hair was tangled about its face. Water ran off its head and shoulders. Its eyes were shut. They snapped open and glowed eerily yellow in the gray evening light. The creature's gaze went from Saul to Shawn and Kelli.

"Quick!" Saul screamed. "The powder. Now! On his head. This is your only chance."

A frightened moan burst from Kelli's throat as her fingers fumbled with the bag. "Oh!" She nearly dropped the bag in the water. If only she could make her hand stop trembling.

Finally, she dug two fingers into the bag and pulled up a clump of gray snake powder. The monster bobbed in the water, hands down at its sides, water still running off its face. It peered at Kelli as if studying her.

Kelli sucked in a deep breath and stretched her hand out. Stretched her hand over the side of the boat. Gripping the chunk of snake powder, she reached her hand over the monster's tangled hair . . .

Stretched as far as she could, leaning over the side of the boat. Held her shaking hand over the monster's head — and let the powder drop.

The monster darted to the right.

The powder drifted down to the water.

MISSED!

Kelli missed. The boat tilted. She felt herself start to fall. With a scream, she toppled out of the boat. Splashed hard into the water. Surprisingly cold. Cold and dark.

She gasped and swallowed water. Choking, she forced herself back up to the surface.

"Nooooo!" She screamed as she saw the monster grab Shawn. The creature wrapped its huge, wet hands under Shawn's armpits, lifted him as if he weighed an ounce, lifted him, kicking and thrashing, out of the boat.

"Noooo!" Kelli cried out again as the monster raised Shawn above his head, spun in the water, sending up a high wave, and carried the screaming boy away.

29

Kelli grabbed the side of the boat. Saul lifted her from the water and helped her climb in. She brushed water from her eyes and forehead with both hands, sweeping her drenched hair behind her head.

"Where is he taking Shawn? What are we going to do?" she cried in a shrill, frightened voice.

"Help me! Kelli! Help!"

Shawn's screams were soon drowned out by the loud splashes as the monster stomped across the water. Shawn flailed his arms and kicked and squirmed. But the huge creature was too strong for any escape.

Kelli and Saul squinted into the gray light, rocking with the rowboat in the wake of the heavy footsteps, watching the monster kick up waves.

"He's taking your brother to that lagoon over there," Saul said. He pointed to a stretch of sand that curved into the river.

"What will he do to him?" Kelli cried. "Can we save him? Can we do anything? Should we follow them over there? Should we go for help?" The questions burst out of her, a frantic explosion of words.

Saul narrowed his eyes and appeared to gaze into the distance. Kelli could see that he was thinking hard. "We have no choice now," he said finally. "There's only one way to save your brother."

"What? What is it?" Kelli demanded. "Tell me!"

"We have to call up the Shaggedy," Saul said. "We have to call up the Shaggedy and order it to destroy the other monster."

30

Rowing back to shore took only a few minutes. But it seemed like *days* to Kelli. Squinting into the distance, she could see Shawn on his knees in the sandy lagoon. The monster loomed nearby. She could see its head and shoulders bobbing in the water.

She and Saul jumped out and pulled the boat onto the muddy shore. Kelli was surprised to see that a small crowd had gathered under the trees. They huddled together, murmuring quietly to one another.

Off to the side of the crowd, she spotted Zeke and Decker. They sat cross-legged on the ground, their hands clasped in their laps. They weren't talking. They were watching Saul and Kelli intently.

Kelli shivered, still dripping wet from her fall into the water. Saul pulled her away from the crowd. He reached into his small backpack again and pulled out a plastic bottle. "This is snake blood," he told her. "We can use this to summon the Shaggedy."

He reached again into the backpack and slid out a sheet of black paper. "I come prepared for *anything*," he said. "This time, *I'll* count the droplets."

Kelli held the paper while Saul dripped snake blood on it. He carefully counted fifty drops out loud. Then they both cupped their hands around their mouths and shouted "Here comes the Shaggedy" ten times.

They turned to the water. Kelli could see Shawn on his knees on the sand on the other side. Would the Shaggedy rise up from the river bottom? Would it arrive in time to rescue her brother?

She could barely breathe. Her heart raced so hard, she felt dizzy. She grabbed Saul's arm. "It . . . it isn't working."

The river rolled smoothly, the gentle current sending up low waves. No churning. No swirling. No sign of any creature.

Kelli turned when she saw Zeke and Decker running toward her. Their blue eyes were wide, their expressions serious. They stopped in front of Kelli and Saul. Kelli waited for them to say something, but they didn't say a word.

"What do you want?" she asked impatiently.

"You summoned us," Zeke said.

"Huh?" Kelli stared at them. "What are you *talking* about?"

"WE are the Shaggedy," Zeke said. "And you have summoned us."

"This isn't the time for jokes," Kelli cried. "My brother has been kidnapped by a monster. And you two idiots —"

She stopped with her mouth hanging open as she saw the two boys begin to change.

They leaned against one another. Pressed their blond heads together. And their bodies started to transform. As Kelli and Saul stared in silent amazement, Zeke and Decker melted . . . melted together . . . they disappeared into each other, growing as they combined. Stretching . . . stretching taller and wider.

"Oh, wow. Oh, wow." Kelli murmured in shock.

The two boys melted into a huge, green, lizard-skinned creature. At least eight feet tall with powerful arms and broad shoulders. It opened its jagged-toothed mouth and bellowed in a thunderous voice:

"TOGETHER, WE ARE THE SHAGGEDY!"

31

"I . . . don't believe it," Saul murmured.

Kelli gaped openmouthed at the huge, ugly monster.

The Shaggedy's lizard-skin chest heaved up and down. It gazed at Kelli with watery red eyes.

Behind her, people screamed in fright. She glimpsed some of them running to the trees for safety.

Kelli took a deep breath. She pointed to the lagoon across the water. "Shaggedy —" she cried. "Follow my order. Go rescue my brother from that other monster!"

The Shaggedy grunted in reply. It swung around. It had a long tail like an alligator. As the creature turned, the tail slapped Kelli and nearly knocked her over. She caught her balance and watched it stomp into the water.

Saul shook his head. "I never guessed . . ." he murmured. "I never guessed about those two boys."

Behind her, people shouted and pointed, watching the Shaggedy burst across the river, sending up tall waves on both sides of it. It appeared to *shove* the water out of its way. It reached the lagoon in less than two minutes.

The other monster rose to greet it. Kelli saw Shawn back away in fright.

The Shaggedy leapt at the other creature. Wrapped its massive arms around the creature's waist and tried to squeeze its breath out.

But the monster wriggled free and sent a blazing-hard fist into the Shaggedy's belly.

Kelli gasped as the Shaggedy doubled over in pain. As its head went down, the other monster swung its fist up and landed a punch under the Shaggedy's jaw. The punch was so loud, Kelli heard the *craaaaack* from across the water.

"Shawn — run! Run!" Kelli was screaming without even realizing it. "Shawn — run away!"

But he seemed frozen in fear. He didn't move.

The Shaggedy staggered under the other monster's punches. One more hard punch to the Shaggedy's head — and it dropped in a heap on the sand.

The Shaggedy sprawled on its back on the sand. It didn't move. Ten seconds went by . . . twenty . . . thirty . . .

"The monster must have killed it," Saul whispered, shaking his head. "I'm so sorry, Kelli. We lose. We lose."

135

32

Kelli froze, watching in horror, praying silently for the Shaggedy to move.

The other monster tossed both fists in the air. It leaped up from the water, cheering itself in triumph. Then it turned and lurched forward with its huge arms outstretched, reaching for her brother.

And as it staggered toward Shawn, the Shaggedy moved quickly. It pulled itself up and dove forward, tackled the monster around its legs. Then it flung the creature into the sand.

The creature appeared to wilt. It went limp. The Shaggedy hoisted it high and heaved it across the water. Kelli watched, hands pressed tightly to the sides of her face, as the monster sank. Its body plunged into the water. Its head was the last to sink.

It didn't return.

The Shaggedy lifted Shawn from the sand. It

hoisted Shawn over one shoulder and began to cross the water, stomping hard.

"Oh, wow!" Kelli cried. "Shawn is okay! The Shaggedy saved him!"

She heard people cheering behind her. She turned in time to see her dad come running across the path. The Shaggedy lowered Shawn to the ground. Kelli and her dad wrapped him in a hug at the same time.

"We're okay! We're okay!" Kelli kept repeating.

She turned to face the Shaggedy. The creature stood with its big arms crossed, watching the family celebration. Water dripped off its reptilian legs. Its red eyes stayed on Kelli.

Then it began to change. The body appeared to pull apart. The creature began to split in two. Its sides tilted away from each other. It made a snapping sound as it separated.

Two heads appeared. Four human arms.

In seconds, Zeke and Decker stood in its place, sweeping water from their blond hair. "We tried to scare you away," Zeke told Kelli. "Together, Decker and I are a monster. We can't help it."

"I don't care if you're a monster," Kelli replied. "You saved my brother's life."

"You don't live under the water?" her father asked, his hands on Shawn's shoulders.

"No," Decker answered. "We want to live normal lives. We didn't want to live in the swamp anymore. We didn't want anyone to guess that we were the Shaggedy. We live in a house. We go to school. We try to act like normal humans. But we're a monster and we can't control it."

"We don't know how it happened to us," Zeke said. "We've always been the Shaggedy."

"You two boys are heroes," Ranger Saul chimed in. He frowned at them. "But I have to take you both away."

Kelli gasped. Everyone stared at Saul.

"I'm not who I said I was," Saul told them. "I'm not a crazy swamp hermit who collects snake heads. I'm a federal agent. I've been here on Monster Watch."

Zeke and Decker took a step back.

"Don't worry," Saul told them. "Since you saved Shawn's life, you'll get very good treatment. But it's my job. I have to take you both away to the federal science labs. They are waiting to study you there."

"I . . . don't . . . think so," Zeke said. He and his brother exchanged glances. Then they put their heads together. They leaned against each other and began to change.

They appeared to melt together. Their arms disappeared into their sides. Their heads melded quickly into one giant, lizard-like head.

Kelli and the others stared in amazement as the Shaggedy stood before them again. Its big chest heaved. It curled and uncurled enormous animal fists.

And then it lunged forward — and grabbed Ranger Saul.

Saul uttered a startled cry as the monster wrapped its arms around his waist and lifted him easily off the ground. Saul's hat went flying, and his long white hair tossed up in the air. He kicked and squirmed, but the Shaggedy held him tightly.

The big creature raised Saul over its head. Held him high. Then pulled back its powerful arms, ready to heave the terrified man into the trees.

"Stop! Stop it!" Kelli screamed, and burst in front of the creature.

The Shaggedy hesitated. It held Saul over its head as if he weighed an ounce.

"Put him down!" Kelli shouted. Her voice came out high and shrill. "I called you up. Do you remember? You must listen to me. You must do as I say."

The monster's red eyes locked on Kelli. The big arms pulled back, ready to heave Saul away. Then the Shaggedy let out a long sigh. It lowered Saul to his feet. It took a step back.

It worked! Kelli thought. *The monster obeyed me.*

"Go back where you came from!" she ordered it. "Back into the swamp where you belong."

Would the monster obey her again?

It tossed back its head and let out a deafening roar. Then it stuck both arms out in front of it, ready to grab someone.

It lurched toward Kelli, its eyes flaming and angry.

"Noooo!" Kelli screamed as the Shaggedy reached her.

But to her surprise, it marched right past her. It stomped into the trees, crushing vines and small shrubs beneath its huge feet. In a few seconds, the monster vanished from sight.

Kelli could still hear its thudding footsteps. But then the footsteps faded away. The swamp was silent.

And then everyone there began to cheer. A cheer of triumph.

"Kelli Andersen, Monster Tamer!" Shawn declared.

More cheers and happy cries and laughter.

Her dad swept Kelli off her feet in a hug. And then all three Andersens were wrapped in a long family hug. "What a close call," their dad kept repeating. "But we're all okay now. We're all okay."

He stood back, sweeping a hand over his bald head. "I've made up my mind, you two," he said. "We're not staying here one more day. I'm taking you back to New York City."

Kelli frowned at him. "Awwww, Dad," she moaned. "Do we have to go? It's much more exciting here."

Read the beginning of the Most Wanted list in book #1!

PLANET OF THE LAWN GNOMES

Here's a sneak peek!

1

I know I'm supposed to be careful. I know I'm supposed to be good. But sometimes you have to take a chance and hope no one is watching.

Otherwise, life would be totally boring, right?

My name is Jay Gardener. I'm twelve and sometimes I can't help it — I like a little excitement. I mean, dare me to do something — and it's done.

It's just the way I am. I'm not a bad dude. Sure, I'm in trouble a lot. I've been in some pretty bad trouble. But that doesn't mean I'm a criminal or anything.

Check out these big blue eyes. Are these the eyes of a criminal? No way. And my curly red hair? And the freckles on my nose? You might almost call me *cute*, right?

Okay, okay. Let's not get sickening about it.

My sister, Kayla, calls me Jay Bird because she says I'm as cute as a bird. Kayla is totally weird. Besides, she has the same red hair and blue eyes. So why pick on *me*?

So, okay, I felt this temptation come on. You know what that is. Just a strong feeling that you have to do something you maybe shouldn't do.

I gazed up and down our street. No one around. *Good.* No one to watch me.

The summer trees' leaves shimmered in the warm sunlight. The houses and lawns gleamed so bright, I had to squint. I stepped into the shade of Mr. McClatchy's front yard.

McClatchy lives in the big old house across the street from us. He's a mean dude and everyone hates him. He's bald and red-faced and as skinny as a toothpick. He wears his pants way up high so the belt is almost up to his armpits.

He yells at everyone in his high, shrill voice. He's always chasing kids off his lawn — even new kids, like Kayla and me. He's even mean to our dog, the sweetest golden Lab who ever lived — Mr. Phineas.

So, I had an idea to have a little fun. Of course it was wrong. Of *course* it wasn't what I was supposed to be doing. But sometimes, when you see something funny to do — you just have to take a chance.

Am I right?

That morning, I saw some guys in green uniforms doing work on the tall trees in McClatchy's front yard. When they went home, they left a ladder leaning against a tree.

I glanced up and down the street again. Still no one in sight.

I crept up to the ladder and grabbed its sides. I slid it away from the tree trunk. The ladder was tall but light. Not hard to move.

Gripping it tightly by the sides, I dragged it to the front of McClatchy's house. I leaned it against the wall. Then I slid it to the open window on the second floor.

Breathing hard, I wiped my sweaty hands on the legs of my jeans. "Sweet," I murmured. "When McClatchy comes home, he'll see the ladder leaning up against the open window. And he'll totally panic. He'll think a burglar broke into his house."

The idea made me laugh. I have a weird laugh. It sounds more like hiccupping than laughing. Whenever I laugh, my whole family starts to laugh because my laugh is so strange.

Well, actually, Mom and Dad haven't been laughing with me much lately. Maybe I've done some things that aren't funny. Maybe I've done some things I shouldn't have. That's why I had to promise to be good and stay out of trouble.

But the ladder against the open window was definitely funny. And it wasn't such a bad thing to do, right? Especially since McClatchy is the meanest, most-hated old dude in the neighborhood.

Still laughing about my joke, I turned and started down the driveway. McClatchy has a tall hedge along the bottom of his yard. It's like a wall. I guess he really wants to keep people out.

At the end of the driveway, his mailbox stood on a tilted pole. And as I passed it, I saw the trash cans in the street. The trash was bulging up under the lids — and it gave me another cool idea.

Working fast, I pulled open the mailbox, lifted the lid off a trash can — and started to stuff trash into McClatchy's mailbox.

Yes! A greasy bag of chicken bones. A crushed soup can. Some gooey yellow stuff that looked like puke. Wet newspapers. More soup cans.

I imagined McClatchy squeaking and squealing in his high voice when he opened the mailbox and found it jammed with disgusting garbage.

What a hoot.

I started to laugh again — but quickly stopped. A choking sound escaped my throat.

Whoa.

Someone watching me. *Two* people watching, half-hidden by the tall hedge.

I froze. They stood side by side, staring right at me. I knew they saw everything. *Everything.*

A chunk of moldy cheese and a clump of newspaper fell from my hands. I staggered back from the mailbox.

Caught. I was totally caught.

About the Author

R.L. Stine's books are read all over the world. So far, his books have sold more than 300 million copies, making him one of the most popular children's authors in history. Besides Goosebumps, R.L. Stine has written the teen series Fear Street and the funny series Rotten School, as well as the Mostly Ghostly series, The Nightmare Room series, and the two-book thriller *Dangerous Girls*. R.L. Stine lives in New York with his wife, Jane, and Minnie, his King Charles spaniel. You can learn more about him at www.RLStine.com.

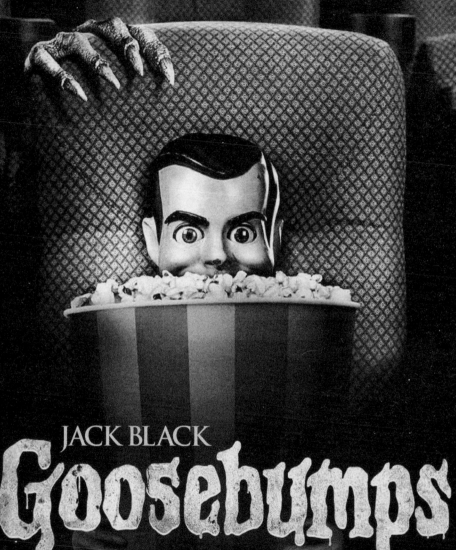

THE SCARIEST PLACE ON EARTH!

Catch the MOST WANTED Goosebumps® villains UNDEAD OR ALIVE!

SPECIAL EDITIONS